LAZY

CALM

SCARY

TOUGH

BANAL

TROPEN VERLAG

sumptuous fire of the stars

SAM SAMORE

verschwen-derisches funkeln der sterne

Fairy tales / Märchen

Return of the Garden was published under another title and different version in *Heart of Darkness*, a catalogue for a group exhibition curated by Marianne Brouwer and produced by the Kröller-Müller Museum, Otterlo. The exhibition took place December 18, 1994 – March 27, 1995. The catalogue was published in February 1997.

Return of the Garden wurde bereits in einer anderen Fassung und unter anderem Titel in *Heart of Darkness* veröffentlicht, einem Katalog zu einer Gruppenausstellung, kuratiert von Marianne Brouwer, herausgegeben vom Kröller-Müller Museum in Otterlo. Diese Ausstellung fand vom 18. Dezember 1994 – 27. März 1995 statt. Der Katalog wurde im Februar 1997 publiziert.

Copyright
© 1998 by Sam Samore and Tropen Verlag, Köln
All rights reserved / Alle Rechte vorbehalten

Cover photo / Umschlagfoto
© 1998 by Sam Samore

German translation / Deutsche Übersetzung
Michael Zöllner

Copy editor / Lektorat
Karl Georg Cadenbach, Christian Ruzicska

A special edition with a photo work from Sam Samore
appears in conjunction with this book,
slip case, numbered and signed, 1-25, 5 A. P.

This special edition is available from all bookshops
and can also be directly ordered from the publisher.
ISBN 3-932170-19-9

Zu diesem Buch erscheint eine Vorzugsausgabe
mit einer Fotoarbeit von Sam Samore,
Schuber, numeriert und signiert, 1-25, 5 E. A.

Die Vorzugsausgabe kann im Buchhandel
oder beim Verlag direkt bestellt werden.
ISBN 3-932170-19-9

Design and typesetting by Tropen Verlag /
Gestaltung und Satz Tropen Verlag, Köln

Printed by / Druck
Farbo Druck, Köln

Printed in Germany

ISBN 3-932170-14-8

Contents / Inhalt

The Tale of … / Die Erzählung von …
9

The Struggle of I / Der Kampf des Ich
13

Return of the Garden / Rückkehr des Gartens
23

The Gift / Das Geschenk
33

Blind Man's Bluff / Blindekuh
47

Queen of the Jungle / Königin des Dschungels
59

Brothers and Sisters / Brüder und Schwestern
71

Birth of a Poet / Geburt eines Dichters
91

Acknowledgment / Anmerkungen
96

precarious grip
on existence
hoard of the
spineless
going at it blind
derisive spit of
glee
without specific
features
death pregnant

The Tale / Die Erzählung

of / von

Sappho,

Mary Shelley,

Herman Melville,

Lady Shonagon,

Homer,

Joseph Conrad,

Geoffrey Chaucer,

Nefertiti,

Alma Mahler,

Giovanni Boccaccio

and Death… / und Tod…

high stillness of
the primeval sea
tribulations of
endless
adolescence
velvet, super-
stitious dread
speech of a
mother
first prayers

S hip slowly sinking. Down down down. No life boats. Lifejackets yes. But consider the setting. The South Pole on the eve of winter. About midnight. Who can survive the freezing ocean's caress? Mary Shelley, Herman Melville, Lady Shonagon, Homer, Joseph Conrad, Sappho, Geoffrey Chaucer, Nefertiti, Giovanni Boccaccio, Alma Mahler and Death, are among the ship's passengers. Mary Shelley asks Death to delay the vessel's sliding hastily under. The group especially assembled for another evening of storytelling. "I permit each one yarn. Whoever tells the best, lives," smirks the toothless Reaper.

Here is their collection of stories. Drawing straws, Sappho goes first with her tale of *The Struggle of I...*

S chiff sinkt langsam. Tiefer tiefer tiefer. Keine Rettungsboote. Schwimmwesten schon. Aber bedenke den Schauplatz. Der Südpol kurz vor Wintereinbruch. Gegen Mitternacht. Wer kann die Liebkosung des gefrierenden Ozeans überleben? Mary Shelley, Herman Melville, Lady Shonagon, Homer, Joseph Conrad, Sappho, Geoffrey Chaucer, Nefertiti, Giovanni Boccaccio, Alma Mahler und Tod sind unter den Passagieren des Schiffs. Mary Shelley bittet Tod, das eilige Hinabgleiten des Dampfers aufzuschieben. Die Gruppe gerade versammelt zu einem weiteren Erzählabend. »Jeder darf einmal sein Garn spinnen. Wer am besten erzählt, lebt«, grient der zahnlose Sensenmann.

Hier ist die Sammlung ihrer Geschichten. Sappho zieht den kürzeren und ist als erste dran, mit ihrer Erzählung *Der Kampf des Ich...*

ghosts with sickly
smiles
capacious
harmony of tones
provocatively
aloof behavior
reason outside
reason
idealistic of
the world

The Struggle of I /
Der Kampf des Ich

precipice of moral
valor
resolute design
prodigious peal of
laughter
instincts of
ordinary cooking
flood gates of the
wonder world
dazzling powers

Once. Four other times. Lived a Roman. Yearning. Her creativity profound. Aspiring. No copyist. Questing. Greater than Athena. A true genius. Named Minerva. Her tapestries exalted. The stuff of legend. Her labors divine. She flesh and blood. Like none other living.

Minerva speaking.

"Call me no progeny of Athena. Let her descend from the heavens unconspiring. Let Athena contest me without mighty History by her side. If she wins by the grace of her own merit. She is superior."

Changing into another form. Not quite this. Not certainly that. Displaying outlines impossible to discern. Athena entered the dream of Minerva. While she lay sleeping.

Athena speaking.

"Ignore not what I say. Celebrate your heritage. Show pride in your genes. Marvel at your education. Do no challenge to the goddess."

Minerva speaking.

"Perhaps your wisdom comes from an ancient place? I am a modern. I am beholden to none. I invent myself on my own. If Athena is fair. If she is honest. Let contrast her talents against mine."

"Indeed she will," pronounced Athena, no longer in disguise.

Everyone bows in homage. Everyone manifests reverence. Every-

Einst. Vor vier Zeiten. Lebte eine Römerin. Sehnsüchtig. Mit tiefer Schöpferkraft. Ehrgeizig. Keine Kopistin. Suchend. Größer als Athene. Ein wahres Genie. Minerva genannt. Ihre Teppiche erhaben. Der Stoff aus dem Legenden sind. Ihre Arbeiten göttlich. Sie aus Fleisch und Blut. Wie keine andere Sterbliche.

Minerva spricht.

»Nennt mich nicht Nachkomme der Athene. Soll sie freimütig vom Himmel herabsteigen. Soll Athene sich mit mir messen, ohne die mächtige Geschichte auf ihrer Seite. Wenn sie durch die Gnade ihrer eigenen Vortrefflichkeit gewinnt. Ist sie überlegen.«

Übergang in eine andere Form. Nicht gerade diese. Nicht genau jene. Umrisse darstellen, die nicht wahrzunehmen sind. Athene erschien Minerva im Traum. Während sie schlafend dalag.

Athene spricht.

»Ignoriere nicht, was ich sage. Feiere dein Erbe. Zeige Stolz in deinen Genen. Staune über deine Erziehung. Fordere die Göttin nicht heraus.«

Minerva spricht.

»Vielleicht stammt deine Weisheit aus einer vergangenen Zeit? Ich bin aus einer modernen. Ich bin niemandem verpflichtet. Ich er-

trembling with
elegance
noiseless twilight
dauntless and
wild desire
social ballast of
competition
staring at the
benign immensity
small courage

one exudes the unctuous. Everyone except Minerva. Undaunted. Smiling resolutely.

Without delay, the two proceed to the contest hall. Each gathers a gossamer strand, forming a web on the beam. The slender shuttle passes to and fro, to and fro, to and fro among the net of threads. Their strong nimble hands make the interlacing effortless. The division of subtle and varied colors without seam.

Regard Athena's tapestry.

The central tondo weaves the scene of her rivalry with Poseidon. Famous schism. Who shall venerate the wisdom of Homer? Who shall celebrate the poetics of Sappho? Who shall lament the death of Socrates? Who shall preside over the birth of Alexander?

Poseidon, ruler of the sea, smites the ground with his trident. A horse erupts from the bowels of the earth. The warrior stallion his gift. Snorting virile. Strutting zealous.

Athena caresses the soil with her wand. An olive tree springs up full grown. Laden with berries. A silent, gentle sapling. Pregnant with repeatable harvest. Chosen transcendent. Athena begins the cult of the Great Mother.

Spiraling out from this tondo are four corners, each representing the

schaffe mich aus mir selber. Wenn Athene gerecht ist. Wenn sie ehrlich ist. Soll sie ihre Talente an meinen messen.«

»Das wird sie«, verkündete Athene, nicht länger verhüllt.

Alle verbeugen sich in Ehrfurcht. Alle bezeugen Respekt. Alle geben sich salbungsvoll. Alle, außer Minerva. Unerschrocken. Entschlossen lächelnd.

Ohne Verzögerung begeben sich die beiden zur Wettkampfstätte. Jede nimmt einen Strang Zwirn und knüpft ein Netz im Webebaum. Das Schiffchen fährt hin und her, hin und her, hin und her im Gewebe der Fäden. Ihren starken, flinken Fingern scheint das Flechten mühelos. Das Absetzen feiner und mannigfaltiger Farben ohne Saum.

Betrachte Athenes Teppich.

Das zentrale Tondo webt die Geschichte ihrer Rivalität mit Poseidon. Behrühmter Streit. Wer wird die Weisheit Homers würdigen? Wer wird die Verse Sapphos feiern? Wer wird den Tod des Sokrates beklagen? Wer wird die Geburt Alexanders überliefern?

Poseidon, Herrscher der Meere, durchbohrt den Grund mit seinem Dreizack. Ein Pferd bricht aus dem Innern der Erde hervor. Das Kriegsroß sein Geschenk. Männlich schnaubend. Aufrecht stolzierend.

Athene schmeichelt der Erde mit ihrem Stab. Ein ausgewachsener

no permanent
plop of habitat
beautiful and
marvelous things
privileges of class
swallowed by the
whirlpool
recovering the
community of
people

displeasure of Mythology when mortals seek change. Giving Minerva fair warning. Capitulate. Surrender. Before it is too late.

Otherwise: Audacious Queen of the Pygmies becomes the crane. Pretentious Antigone turns into the stork.

Regard Minerva's tapestry.

Her designs show the treacheries of the male pantheon. As a graceful swan, Zeus dupes the unsuspecting Leda. As rays of golden light, Zeus penetrates Danae's fortified tower. As a gentle bull, Zeus gallops away with naive Europa on his back. Taking her to the sea. Far away from her home. Ravishing her. Satisfying his unquenchable lust.

Zeus the only contriver? A thousand times no. Poseidon changes into a fierce bull, fooling the goddess Ceres. Poseidon transforms into a gentle horse, betraying Medusa. Poseidon metamorphoses himself, intending always to deceive.

Athena's judgment?

Jealousy decrees Minerva's tapestry a work of art sublime. Envy torments. Indignation rages. Admiration hisses. In a fury, Athena swallows up whole Minerva's representation. Triumphantly she kisses Minerva three times, then four times. Minerva flees the contest room. Confused by desire. Filled with outrage.

Olivenbaum schießt empor. Beladen mit Früchten. Ein stiller, zarter Schößling. Trächtig mit wiederkehrender Ernte. Vortrefflich ausgewählt. Athene beginnt mit dem Kult der Großen Mutter.

Diesem Tondo entwinden sich vier Ausläufer, jeder stellt den Verdruß der Mythologie dar, wenn Sterbliche aufbegehren. Deutliche Warnung an Minerva. Gib auf. Unterwirf dich. Bevor es zu spät ist.

Sonst: Die überhebliche Königin der Pygmäen wird zum Kranich. Die anmaßende Antigone verwandelt sich in einen Storch.

Betrachte Minervas Teppich.

Ihre Muster zeigen die Treulosigkeiten des männlichen Pantheon. Als anmutiger Schwan täuscht Zeus die arglose Leda. Als goldener Regen dringt Zeus in Danaes befestigten Turm ein. Als zutraulicher Stier galoppiert Zeus mit der nichtsahnenden Europa auf seinem Rücken davon. Bringt sie zum Meer. Weit weg von ihrem Zuhause. Schändet sie. Befriedigt seine unstillbare Lust.

Zeus als einziger Erfinder? Tausendmal Nein. Poseidon wird zu einem wilden Stier, um die Göttin Ceres zu täuschen. Poseidon wechselt in ein zutrauliches Pferd, um Medusa zu trügen. Poseidon verwandelt sich immer nur aus Hinterlist.

Athenes Urteil?

crying with fear
doing something
very bad
the meanness, the
planning, the
discontent
hunger and fear
breeding rage
standing silently
and watching

Finding Minerva hanging by her long refined neck on the beams of the temple, Athena cries out, "You shall weave for eternity!" With the juices of her saliva, Athena massages Minerva's body. Her nose and ears shrivel. Her appendages adhere to her torso. Her fingers grow into hairy legs.

Minerva's dream never ended.

Still today she gracefully spins her marvelous tapestries! With the same genius! With the same beauty! As when Athena touched her, and transformed her into the spider.

■

Eifersucht erklärt Minervas Teppich zum erhabenen Kunstwerk. Neid bohrt. Entrüstung tobt. Bewunderung zischt. In ihrer Wut schluckt Athena Minervas ganze Darstellung herunter. Triumphierend küßt sie Minerva erst dreimal, dann viermal. Minerva flieht den Austragungsort. Verwirrt von Verlangen. Völlig aufgebracht.

Als Athene Minerva findet, mit ihrem langen, schlanken Hals am Gebälk des Tempels hängend, ruft sie aus: »Du sollst weben bis in alle Ewigkeit!« Mit den Säften ihres Gaumens massiert Athene Minervas Körper. Ihre Nase und Ohren schrumpfen. Ihre Gliedmaßen verschmelzen mit dem Körper. Ihre Finger wachsen zu haarigen Beinen.

Minervas Traum hat niemals geendet.

Bis heute spinnt sie kunstvoll ihre wunderbaren Teppiche! Mit derselben Begabung! Mit derselben Schönheit! Wie damals, als Athene sie berührte und sie in eine Spinne verwandelte.

■

utterances of
inspired
prophetesses
kindness bundled
by sin
imbecile sound in
the almighty
emptiness
confessions of
bestiality

Return of the Garden/
Rückkehr des Gartens

succumbing to
mysticism
immense coiling
serpent
blaring the silky
quagmire
striking angels
with stones
speaking to the
eternal time

A wife. A husband. A son, Rafik. Living in the desert. Some where. Some other time.

Six poor goats live too.

Rafik turns twelve. His father dies. He assumes all the chores. He awakens every dawn. He milks the goats. He stews a meal of rice and beans for his mother each noon. He cleans the ashes from the fire. He tidies their dilapidated tent. He shepherds the goats to the pasture far away. He collapses into bed late at night, ragged clothes clinging to his gaunt body.

A year later.

Rafik's mother marries again. His new stepfather, bringing three sons, does not want to labor. Nor do his sons.

Monday afternoon.

While Rafik tends the goats on the small patch of weeds, a long green snake slithers up. Emerging from the cosmos underground. Startling Rafik.

The snake clears her throat, then declares in a slinky voice, "The Hunters are chasing me. I need a place to hide. If they find me, they will kill me."

Rafik swallows the serpent. The Hunters appear. Rafik leaks not a

Eine Frau. Ein Mann. Ein Sohn, Rafik. Leben in der Wüste. Irgendwo. Irgendwann.

Sechs dürre Ziegen leben auch.

Rafik wird zwölf. Sein Vater stirbt. Er übernimmt die täglichen Pflichten. Er erwacht im Morgengrauen. Er melkt die Ziegen. Er bereitet für seine Mutter jeden Mittag eine Mahlzeit aus Reis und Bohnen. Er reinigt die Feuerstelle. Er macht sauber in ihrem heruntergekommenen Zelt. Er führt die Ziegen auf die weit entfernte Weide. Er sinkt tief in der Nacht erschöpft ins Bett, die zerlumpte Kleidung klebt an seinem mageren Körper.

Ein Jahr später.

Rafiks Mutter heiratet wieder. Sein neuer Stiefvater, er hat drei Söhne, will nicht arbeiten. Seine Söhne auch nicht.

Montag nachmittag.

Während Rafik die Ziegen auf einem schmalen Streifen Unkraut hütet, gleitet eine lange, grüne Schlange heran. Sie kommt aus der kosmischen Unterwelt. Und erschreckt Rafik.

Die Schlange räuspert sich, erklärt dann in schleppendem Tonfall: »Die Jäger verfolgen mich. Ich muß mich verstecken. Wenn sie mich finden, werden sie mich töten.«

the unfathomable
sky and earth
enrapturing
freedom of action
way of solitude
powers of
metamorphosis
shifting of
silence
sleeping cows

word. The Hunters disappear.

The serpent slides out of his mouth. Chakra is her name. Chakra the snake spirit. She thanks Rafik. He saved her life. She offers to help him in return. "Make one request now!" Chakra laughs.

Rafik wishes for a plentiful garden. On the very spot they stand. He covets a place filled with aromatic jasmine, shady palm trees, luscious pears, scrumptious dates. Lots of grass for the goats!

In the blink of an eye, the oasis materializes.

Rafik and his goats frolic in the weald. Feasting in rapturous delight. Lounging on the soft fertile meadow.

Not a worry in the world.

On the afternoon of the fourth day. A soldier on galloping camel speeds through the grove. In terror, the goats flee. Rafik chases after his flock. As he starts running out of the island, it follows along with him. He never leaves the forest's boundaries. He remains always within its domain.

The moving oasis enchants the soldier. Rafik recounts the curious tale. The young lieutenant is a princess from another land. Rafik and the princess become intimate friends. Rafik decides to live with her people. The paradise follows along.

Rafik verschluckt die Schlange. Die Jäger erscheinen. Rafik verrät nicht ein Wort. Die Jäger verschwinden.

Die Schlange gleitet aus seinem Mund. Chakra heißt sie. Sie dankt Rafik. Er hat ihr das Leben gerettet. Sie bietet ihm dafür ihre Hilfe an. »Wünsch dir jetzt etwas!« Chakra lacht.

Rafik wunscht sich einen wunderbaren Garten. An genau dem Ort, an dem sie stehen. Er begehrt einen Ort, gefüllt mit duftendem Jasmin, schattenspendenden Palmenbäumen, süßen Birnen, köstlichen Datteln. Genügend Gras für die Ziegen!

In einem einzigen Augenblick entsteht die Oase.

Rafik und seine Ziegen tollen ausgelassen in der Hügellandschaft herum. Weiden sich in ekstatischen Wonnen. Faulenzen auf der weichen, saftigen Wiese.

Keine einzige Sorge auf der Welt.

Am Nachmittag des vierten Tages. Ein Krieger auf einem gallopierenden Kamel sprengt durch den Graben. Die Ziegen fliehen in Panik. Rafik setzt seiner Herde nach. Als er versucht, die Insel zu verlassen, folgt sie ihm auf dem Fuße. Er überschreitet niemals die Grenzen des Waldes. Er bleibt immer innerhalb seines Gebietes.

Die wandernde Oase erheitert den Krieger. Rafik erzählt die denk-

proud exiles from
tyranny
circling the
infernos
tears of genuine
laughter
voices of the surf
humbling
through grief
bed of nails

As a wedding gift, Rafik's stepfather sends jellied fruits with his mother. The stepfather laces them with venom. It is a strenuous journey from the poor tribe to the neighboring country. On the way Rafik's mother rests beside a well. She falls asleep for a few hours. Out of the hole in the ground comes Chakra, the long green snake. She devours all the poison.

When the mother arrives. When the mother presents the gift. When Rafik eats the fruit. He does not die.

The stepfather makes a batch of poisoned bread. Again, Rafik's mother falls asleep beside the circle of water. Again Chakra swallows the toxin from the bread. Again Rafik does not die.

The incensed stepfather plots and waits.

Rafik gives birth to a child in June. The stepfather asks for the baby. It must be baptized in their village. Honoring the request, Rafik and the baby trek to the family.

Exhausted by the lengthy Hegira, Rafik and the baby take an early evening nap. The stepfather picks up the sleeping Rafik. The stepfather throws him into a deep chasm. Rafik falls a vast distance. Descends a long, long, long way.

The stepfather dispatches his three sons to wed the princess.

würdige Geschichte. Der junge Leutnant ist eine Prinzessin aus einem anderen Land. Rafik und die Prinzessin werden enge Freunde. Rafik entschließt sich, bei ihrem Volk zu leben. Das Paradies kommt mit.

Als Hochzeitsgeschenk gibt Rafiks Stiefvater der Mutter eingelegte Früchte mit. Der Stiefvater glasiert sie mit Gift. Es ist eine anstrengende Reise von dem armen Stamm zum benachbarten Land. Auf dem Weg ruht sich Rafiks Mutter an einer Quelle aus. Sie schläft für ein paar Stunden ein. Aus der Öffnung im Boden kommt Chakra, die lange, grüne Schlange. Sie verschlingt das ganze Gift.

Als die Mutter ankommt. Als sie die Geschenke überreicht. Als Rafik die Früchte ißt. Stirbt er nicht.

Der Stiefvater backt einen ganzen Schub vergiftetes Brot. Wieder schläft Rafiks Mutter neben dem Wasserrund ein. Wieder schluckt Chakra das Gift des Brotes. Wieder stirbt Rafik nicht.

Der wütende Stiefvater macht neue Pläne und wartet.

Rafik bekommt im Juni ein Kind. Der Stiefvater verlangt nach dem Kind. Es soll in ihrem Dorf getauft werden. Rafik entspricht der Bitte und wandert mit dem Neugeborenen zu seiner Familie.

Erschöpft von der langwierigen Hedschra legen sich Rafik und das Neugeborene schon am frühen Abend schlafen. Der Stiefvater nimmt

momentary
bemusement
hatless, coatless,
wiskered
more real and less
illusionary
thriftless and
uncareful families
errors of greed
his soul in danger

They bring back the baptized baby.

In the autumn while the princess sits on the terrace, reading *The Thousand Nights and One Night*, she hears a voice coming from a nearby cavern. The voice of Rafik.

But it has a strange, slinky sound. With each passing minute, the voice moves closer and closer towards the cave's entrance.

Rafik appears. He is a long green snake. He explains to the princess why he married Chakra. The princess understands. They both promise to meet every day, for as long as they live.

This is not the end of the story. From the sky fall four apples. One for you. One for me. One for Chakra, the snake spirit.

■

den schlafenden Rafik. Der Stiefvater wirft ihn einen tiefen Abgrund hinunter. Rafik fällt unermeßlich tief. Stürzt eine lange, lange, lange Strecke hinab.

Der Stiefvater schickt seine drei Söhne los, um die Prinzessin zu heiraten. Sie bringen das getaufte Neugeborene zurück.

Als die Prinzessin im Herbst auf der Terasse sitzt und *Geschichten aus tausendundeiner Nacht* liest, hört sie eine Stimme aus einer nahegelegenen Höhle. Die Stimme von Rafik.

Aber sie hat einen fremden, schleppenden Unterton. Mit jeder Minute, die vorübergeht, kommt die Stimme näher und näher zum Eingang der Höhle.

Rafik erscheint. Er ist eine lange, grüne Schlange. Er erklärt der Prinzessin, warum er Chakra geheiratet hat. Die Prinzessin versteht. Die beiden versprechen einander, sich jeden Tag zu treffen, solange sie leben.

Das ist nicht das Ende der Geschichte. Vom Himmel fallen vier Äpfel herab. Einer für dich. Einer für mich. Einer für Chakra, den Schlangengeist.

■

lost in boundless
disarray
catalytic
combustion of
recollections
to the bottom of
the well
absence of any
guile
loyal dogs

The Gift /
Das Geschenk

fable-mongering
lips
sleeping in the
skin
return from some
bloody nowhere
masterly
achievement of
lying
pecking birds

Every September Coyote and his friend Iktome climb up the lofty turquoise Mesa. They come to leave an offering. They rub shoulders with the Clouds. And pay their respects to the Sun.

It's their ritual.

Every year they stop for a chat with Baa. Baa the Boulder. Baa has extraordinary memory. Baa is beautiful. Baa is clairvoyant. Baa is formidable.

"Greetings friend Baa!" smiled Coyote. "You radiate happiness in the morning sunrise. You deserve a gift. Let my blanket adorn you. You'll feel warm during the long winter nights."

"That's generous of you, Coyote," blinked Iktome.

"Baa exudes a regal splendiferousness wearing that blanket of mine."

"You mean *his* blanket," winked Iktome.

The two pals continued their climb towards the top of the mesa. But it grew frostier, blew windier. Blue sky forged dark gray. Icy rain plopped down upon their heads. Sleet curled into large pellets of ice.

The two scampered to a nearby *kiva*. A chilly, damp and leaky *kiva*. Iktome felt plenty warm. He remembered to bring along his furry cape.

Jedes Jahr im September besteigen Kojote und sein Freund Iktome den gewaltigen, türkisen Tafelberg. Sie kommen, um ein Opfer zu bringen. Sie reiben ihre Schultern an den Wolken. Und zollen der Sonne ihren Respekt.

Das ist ihr Ritual.

Jedes Jahr halten sie auf ein Schwätzchen bei Baa. Baa dem Felsbrocken. Baa hat ein ausgezeichnetes Gedächtnis. Baa sieht prächtig aus. Baa kann hellsehen. Baa ist unbezwingbar.

»Grüß dich, Freund Baa!«, grinste Kojote. »Du verstrahlst schon bei Sonnenaufgang Freude. Du verdienst ein Geschenk. Meine Decke soll dich schmücken. Du wirst es warm haben während der langen Winternächte.«

»Das ist großzügig von dir«, blinzelte Iktome.

»Baa strahlt mit meiner Decke eine königliche Würde aus.«

»Du meinst mit *seiner* Decke«, zwinkerte Iktome.

Die zwei Kumpane setzten ihren Aufstieg zum Gipfel des Tafelbergs fort. Aber es wurde frostiger, blies windiger. Blauer Himmel wich dunklem Grau. Eisiger Regen prasselte ihnen auf die Köpfe. Graupel verdichtete sich zu dicken Hagelkörnern.

Die beiden flüchteten zu einer nahegelegenen *Kiva*. Eine zugige,

the wanderer's
deliriums
slackness of jaw
powered only by
fiction
supernatural wind
sickness rioting
the soil
caress of fortune
buffooning pigs

Coyote only wore his velour costume. Nothing else. He had given his blanket to Baa. What was he going to do? His jaws started to chatter, chatter, chatter, chatter. Goose bumps sprouted up all over his body. Teary eyed Coyote sneezed! Red nosed Coyote coughed!

"My dear," pleaded Coyote. "Help me out! Ask Baa for that covering of mine. He doesn't need it! He's been alive on this planet for millennia. Go with great speed! I'm turning into an icicle."

Iktome did the favor. Rushing to the Boulder.

"Baa. Comrade! As an extra-special-emergency-request! We need the quilt! Coyote's turned the color of Polar Bear!"

"Never can gifts be returned," intoned Baa.

Iktome told Coyote the news.

"Selfish Boulder! He doesn't deserve my hospitality! I have no other choice. I refuse to give him my afghan again!" barked Coyote.

"Brother. Listen to me. Baa has magic. Respect his feelings."

"What do you mean? Who do you think you're talking to? I am Coyote! My blanket is rapturously exquisite. Snugly warm! It smells of honey. I'm going to tell Baa how much he's hurt my feelings."

When Coyote asked for the covering, solemn Baa replied, "Must you adopt the ways of the White Man?"

feuchte und tropfende *Kiva*. Iktome war es angenehm warm. Er hatte daran gedacht, seinen Pelzumhang mitzunehmen.

Kojote trug nur seinen Veloursanzug. Sonst nichts. Seine Decke hatte er Baa gegeben. Was sollte er machen? Seine Zähne begannen zu klappern, klappern, klappern, klappern. Er bekam am ganzen Körper Gänsehaut. Mit tränenden Augen nieste Kojote! Mit roter Nase hustete Kojote!

»Mein Bester«, flehte Kojote. »Hilf mir! Frag Baa nach meiner Decke. Er braucht sie nicht! Er lebt seit Jahrtausenden auf diesem Planeten. Geh, spute dich! Ich verwandle mich sonst in einen Eiszapfen.«

Iktome tat ihm den Gefallen. Er eilte zum Felsbrocken.

»Baa. Kamerad! Eine Super-Sonder-Notfall-Bitte! Wir brauchen die Steppdecke! Kojote hat schon die Farbe eines Eisbären angenommen!«

»Geschenke kann man nicht zurückgeben«, intonierte Baa.

Iktome brachte Kojote die Nachricht.

»Egoistischer Felsbrocken! Er verdient meine Freundschaft nicht! Ich habe keine andre Wahl. Ich weigere mich, ihm meinen Afganen noch einmal zu geben!«, bellte Kojote.

»Bruder. Hör mir zu. Baa besitzt magische Kräfte. Respektiere seine Gefühle.«

dreaming fantasy
to the outlines
ferocious biting
and swallowing
secrets of the
universe
merry caper of life
optimism induced
by hallucination
stubborn hens

"Can't you imagine my situation?! The blanket is mine! Where's your power now, Baa?!" taunted Coyote, scooting off with the quilt.

Coyote ran back to the *kiva*. A grin of triumph on his face. There Coyote and Iktome rested. Warm and content.

By the end of the afternoon, the rain and hail and snow disappeared. Sun popped out of the Clouds. The air smelled fresh.

Coyote and Iktome emerged from the *kiva* to gobble up their delicious lunch. The two stretched out lazily on the meadow. It was a heavenly afternoon.

Suddenly Iktome bolted upright and whispered, "Shhh. I hear something."

"What are you talking about?"

"I hear a sound. It's heading our way."

"Hmmm. You're right. Like distant drumbeats."

"Could be an avalanche. We're going to be buried alive!"

Then they saw the Boulder. Baa. Scratching, pounding, snorting, growling. Baa heading straight for Coyote!

"We're in profound trouble!" yelled Coyote.

"Baa's going to massacre us!" screamed Iktome.

The two pranksters galloped away in a frenzy. But the Boulder

»Was soll das heißen? Was glaubst du, mit wem du sprichst? Ich bin Kojote! Meine Decke ist außerordentlich exquisit. Mollig warm! Sie riecht nach Honig. Ich werde Baa sagen, wie sehr er meine Gefühle verletzt hat.«

Als Kojote nach der Decke fragte, antwortete Baa nur: »Mußt du die Gewohnheiten des weißen Mannes annehmen?«

»Kannst du dir meine Situation nicht vorstellen?! Die Decke gehört mir! Wo bleibt deine Macht jetzt, Baa?«, spottete Kojote, während er sich mit der Decke aus dem Staub machte.

Kojote rannte zurück zu der *Kiva*. Ein triumphierendes Grinsen im Gesicht. Dort ruhten sich Kojote und Iktome aus. Warm und zufrieden.

Gegen Ende des Nachmittags ließen Regen und Hagel und Schnee nach. Sonne brach durch die Wolken. Die Luft roch frisch.

Kojote und Iktome verließen die *Kiva*, um gierig ihr köstliches Mittagessen zu verschlingen. Die beiden streckten sich faul auf der Wiese aus. Es war ein himmlischer Nachmittag.

Plötzlich richtete Iktome sich auf und flüsterte: »Psst. Ich höre was.«

»Wovon redest du?«

»Ich höre ein Geräusch. Es kommt auf uns zu.«

symbol of
physical scars
steady piercing
glances
threshold of
profound feelings
heavy with moon
intolerably
excessive bliss
eyes into lips

twisted faster and faster and faster and faster.

They came upon a clear emerald lake. "Jump into the water," panted Iktome. "Baa will sink to the bottom!" They swam across the lake. The Boulder did too! Barreling closer and closer and closer and closer!

They came upon a grove of red Sequoia trees. "Iktome!" howled Coyote. "Run into the forest. Baa can't dodge these giant Sequoias!" After passing through the woods to a field of flowers, they could hear the splintering of timber. Baa smashed down tree after tree after tree after tree into teeny tiny toothpicks.

In wild terror, Coyote and Iktome approached a very flat, very wide, tundra of sagebrush. No trees. No mountains. No water. No valleys. No nothing. Nothing except a prairie expanding across the infinite horizon.

Iktome, who's also known as Spider Man, looked down at the watch on his wrist and gasped, "Ahem. Coyote! Brother. What time is it? Oh no! I must deliver a ceremony at the lodge. I'm already late! You understand!" Iktome quickly changed into a spider and scurried over to the shade of a nearby cactus.

Coyote sprinted off across the desert. Never looking back. Soon he could feel Baa's hot breath singeing the hair of his neck. With a

»Hmmm. Du hast recht. Wie entfernte Trommelschläge.«

»Könnte eine Lawine sein. Wir werden lebendig begraben werden!«

Dann erkannten sie den Felsbrocken. Baa. Krachend, stampfend, schnaufend, grollend. Baa, direkt auf Kojote zukommend!

»Wir stecken in großen Schwierigkeiten!«, kreischte Kojote.

»Baa wird uns massakrieren!«, schrie Iktome.

Die beiden Großmäuler galoppierten mit Entsetzen davon. Aber der Felsbrocken drehte sich schneller und schneller und schneller und schneller.

Sie gelangten an einen klaren, smaragdenen See. »Spring ins Wasser«, keuchte Iktome. »Baa wird zu Boden sinken!« Sie schwammen durch den See. Der Felsbrocken aber auch! Und walzte näher und näher und näher und näher!

Sie kamen an ein Wäldchen mit roten Mammutbäumen. »Iktome!«, heulte Kojote. »Lauf in den Wald. Baa kann nicht um diese gigantischen Mammutbäume herumflitzen!« Nachdem sie aus dem Wald auf eine Blumenwiese gelangt waren, hörten sie das Splittern von Holz. Baa verarbeitete Baum um Baum um Baum um Baum zu klitzekleinen Zahnstochern.

In panischem Entsetzen näherten sich Kojote und Iktome einer

hunting frogs
pleasuring for
sadness
losing backwards
crazy shoutings of
a child
unseemly in a
grown woman
walking around
like a ghost

mighty boom and noisy crunch, Baa mowed down Coyote. Squashing him into a thin pancake.

Baa gathered up the blanket and strolled home, whistling his favorite tune.

A cowboy riding out on the range at sunset, noticed the flattened Coyote and said to himself, "This is a mighty fine carpet. We need one for the living room. It'll be real cozy."

Now the times when Coyote dies, he has enough sorcery to bring himself back to life.

But hold on!

It doesn't happen overnight. Coyote has to be patient. For a few days he lay there, at the foot of the fireplace. On Wednesday, Coyote stood up. People and dogs and all other kinds of creatures had been walking all over him. He dusted himself off. Then he trotted out the front screen door.

Sitting in the dining room, the cowboy's nine-year-old daughter saw the whole thing happen. After Coyote disappeared, she hurried over to her father.

"Hey dad!" she shouted. "Your rug took off without saying good - bye."

außerordentlich flachen, außerordentlich weiten Steppe mit Salbei-büschen. Keine Bäume. Keine Berge. Kein Wasser. Keine Täler. Kein nichts. Nichts, außer einer Prärie, die sich entlang des endlosen Horizonts erstreckte.

Iktome, auch bekannt als Spiderman, schaute herunter auf die Uhr an seinem Knöchel und räusperte sich, »Ähem, Kojote! Bruder. Wieviel Uhr ist es eigentlich? Oh Nein! Ich muß ja noch zu einem Empfang beim Förster. Ich bin schon zu spät! Du verstehst!« Iktome verwandelte sich unverzüglich in eine Spinne und krabbelte in den Schatten eines nahegelegen Kaktus.

Kojote sprintete los in die Wüste. Ohne zurückzuschauen. Bald schon konnte er Baas heißen Atem in seinem Nacken spüren. Mit einem mächtigen Dröhnen und geräuschvollem Schmatzen mähte Baa Kojote nieder. Drückte ihn platt zu einem dünnen Pfannkuchen.

Baa rollte die Decke zusammen und schlenderte, sein Lieblingslied pfeifend, nach Hause.

Einem Cowboy, der bei Sonnenuntergang seinen Ausritt machte, fiel der geplättete Kojote auf, und er sagte bei sich: » Das ist ein prächtiger kleiner Teppich. Wir brauchen noch einen fürs Wohnzimmer. Das wird gemütlich werden.«

making a rock out
of a piece of paper
murderer halving
the wizard
strange and lovely
disintegration
mesmerizing
old man
from loneliness
to horror

"I'll be darned!" he scowled. "I've heard of things like this happening before."

And Coyote? Coyote will always remember what Baa taught him: Never take back what you have given. Yup. That's right. Coyote sure learned his lesson.

Or did he?

■

Allerdings hat Kojote genug Zauberkraft, sich selber wieder zum Leben zu erwecken.

Aber abwarten!

Das passiert nicht über Nacht. Kojote muß geduldig sein. Ein paar Tage lag er da, vor dem Kamin. Am Mittwoch stand Kojote auf. Menschen und Hunde und alle sonstigen Viecher waren über ihn getrampelt. Er schlug sich den Staub ab. Dann trottete er zur Haustür hinaus.

Im Eßzimmer sitzend, beobachtete die neunjährige Tochter des Cowboys das ganze Geschehen. Nachdem Kojote verschwunden war, eilte sie zu ihrem Vater.

»He, Papa!«, rief sie. »Dein Vorleger ist abgehauen, ohne auf Wiedersehen zu sagen.«

»Verflixt und zugenäht!« grummelte er. »Ich habe von solchen Sachen schon gehört.«

Und Kojote? Kojote wird sich immer daran erinnern, was Baa ihm beigebracht hat: Geschenkte Sachen holt man sich nicht zurück. Jups. Das stimmt. Kojote hat seine Lektion sicherlich gelernt.

Das hat er doch?

■

happy expectation
of strangling
smiling the
irrefutable
meaning
delirious
pilgrimage of
sybarites
phobia of spiders
burning impulse

Blind Man's Bluff /
Blindekuh

hidden branches
of the mind
chalice of torment
having no dinner
fear of retaliation
becoming
anonymous
painful
dependence on
someone

Natasha had a son named Peter. She a widowed farmer. They lived with Natasha's sister. She too a widowed farmer. Caring for a son.

Along with the fathers, all the other children disappeared last autumn. No one could explain why. But the neighbors whispered to themselves. Perhaps, they said, Natasha's sister had murdered each one of them for food.

Winters were a terrifying struggle to survive. This January boded as the worst in memory. All of the stored summer crops eaten by the ravens. Starvation haunting. No food to be found.

On the eve of the new moon. While the children slept by the barren fireplace. Natasha's sister snarled, "Take Peter into the woods. Leave him in the clay hut. He must fight the Baba for our survival."

Dawn.

Carrying only a tiny bag of grits. Natasha walked arm in arm with Peter to the mud hovel. She advised, "Build the fire. Never let it die. Cook your porridge after sundown. Spin the straw. Keep the windows closed. The door hinged shut. Do what is good."

Sunset.

Peter had spun all the straw into gold. He boiled the cereal. He

Natascha hatte einen Sohn namens Peter. Sie eine verwitwete Farmerin. Zuammen lebten sie mit Nataschas Schwester. Sie auch eine verwitwete Farmerin. Mit einem Sohn.

Gleichzeitig mit den Vätern verschwanden im letzten Herbst auch alle anderen Kinder. Niemand konnte sagen warum. Aber die Nachbarn tuschelten untereinander. Vielleicht, so sagten sie, hatte Nataschas Schwester sie alle umgebracht, um sie zu essen.

Die Winter waren ein furchtbarer Überlebenskampf. Der Januar war angekündigt als der strengste seit Menschengedenken. Die ganze Sommerernte von den Raben gefressen. Hungertod ging um. Nirgendwo etwas zu essen.

Am Vorabend des Neumonds. Während die Kinder vor dem armseligen Kaminfeuer schliefen. Murrte Nataschas Schwester, »Führ Peter in die Wälder. Laß ihn in der Tonhütte zurück. Er muß zu unserer Rettung gegen den Baba kämpfen«.

Dämmerung.

Nur einen kleinen Beutel mit Schrot bei sich. Ging Natascha Arm in Arm mit Peter zu der Schlammbaracke. Sie wies ihn an, »Mach Feuer. Laß es nicht ausgehen. Koch deinen Haferbrei nach Sonnenuntergang. Spinn Stroh. Halt die Fenster geschlossen. Die Tür fest zu.

pathos of a
pleading murmur
stinking limbs of
torn comrades
longing for action,
not words
days of physical
isolation
disappearing
from sight

lifted the spoon to his cracked lips. From the shadows emerged the black fox, "Child! Feed me a handful of your kasha."

"Dear spirit! Stay beside me in my anguish. I will give you more than one handful. Eat all you desire," lamented Peter.

The black fox ate. The black fox sang Peter lullabies to sleep. The black fox vanished.

Midnight.

The wolf entered, "Child! Blow out the candle. You and I. We play blind man's bluff."

The black fox re-emerged and leapt onto Peter's shoulder, whispering, "Have courage. Snuff the flame. Hide beneath the stove. I shall run and ring the chime."

Peter did as he was told.

The wolf chased the black fox. Round and round. Round and round. The wolf growled fiercely. The wolf thrashed his sharp claws about. The wolf snapped the fangs of his mighty jaws. The wolf could not catch the black fox.

The wolf grew weary, "Child! Gifted player. Abundant food your reward."

Daybreak.

Tue nur, was gut ist«.

Sonnenuntergang.

Peter hatte das ganze Stroh zu Gold gesponnen. Er kochte das Getreide. Er führte den Löffel an seine gesprungenen Lippen. Aus den Schatten löste sich der schwarze Fuchs, »Kind! Füttere mich mit einer Hand voll Kasha«.

»Lieber Geist! Bleib bei mir in meiner Furcht. Ich werde dir mehr als nur eine Hand voll geben. Iß soviel du magst«, jammerte Peter.

Der schwarze Fuchs aß. Der schwarze Fuchs sang Peter zum Einschlafen Wiegenlieder. Der schwarze Fuchs verschwand.

Mitternacht.

Der Wolf trat ein, »Kind! Blas die Kerze aus. Du und ich. Wir spielen Blindekuh«.

Der schwarze Fuchs erschien ebenfalls und sprang auf Peters Schulter, flüsternd, »Sei tapfer. Lösch das Licht. Versteck dich neben dem Herd. Ich werde rennen und ein Glöckchen läuten«.

Peter tat, wie ihm befohlen wurde.

Der Wolf jagte den schwarzen Fuchs. Hin und her. Der Wolf heulte furchterregend. Der Wolf schlug mit seinen scharfen Klauen um sich. Der Wolf schnappte mit den Fängen seines gewaltigen Kiefers. Der

cannibalizing
distress
nothing but water
ink spot of bliss
suffering from
loneliness
breaking away
from the family
lamenting a
ludicrous wail

Natasha's sister spat, "Be quick. Bring Peter to me."

Natasha hurried into the woods. Her tattered shoes crumbling into ribbons of leather. The sister waited near the portal.

Noon.

The dog barked, "Bow-wow. Bow-wow. Natasha and Peter command a team of horses, with a sleigh loaded plentiful."

"Filthy hound! You lie. I hear the jostling of Peter's bones. His flesh soon to be eaten," Natasha's sister scowled a ghoulish jeer.

The horses trotted through the gate. The sister beheld Natasha and Peter sitting on a carriage laden with fruits, vegetables and meats. The sister's eyes gleamed wild with rage.

"What have you brought? Nothing! You, Natasha. Take my son into the forest. He is so much the better! He returns with three teams of horses and three cartfuls of food," cried Natasha's sister.

Dawn.

Natasha lead her sister's son to the gravel hutch.

Sunset.

The son had spun all the straw into gold. He boiled the oats. The black fox appeared, asking for a handful. The son screamed, "Away you evil demon!"

Wolf konnte den schwarzen Fuchs nicht kriegen.

Der Wolf wurde müde, »Kind. Geschickter Spieler. Essen im Überfluß sei deine Belohnung«.

Tagesanbruch.

Nataschas Schwester spuckte, »Beeil dich. Bring Peter zu mir«.

Natascha eilte in die Wälder. Ihre zerlumpten Schuhe lösten sich auf in Lederstreifen. Die Schwester wartete nahe der Pforte.

Mittag.

Der Hund bellte, »Wau-wau. Wau-wau. Natascha und Peter führen ein Pferdegespann mit einem vollbeladenen Schlitten«.

»Dreckiger Bastard! Du lügst. Ich höre das Klappern von Peters Knochen. Sein Fleisch bereit zum Verzehr«, grollte Nataschas Schwester mit kannibalischem Spott.

Die Pferde trotteten durch das Tor. Die Schwester erblickte Natascha und Peter auf einem Wagen, beladen mit Früchten, Gemüse und Fleisch. Die Augen der Schwester funkelten wild vor Zorn.

»Was habt ihr gebracht? Nichts! Du, Natascha. Führ meinen Sohn in den Wald. Er ist viel besser! Er wird mit drei Pferdegespannen und drei Wagenladungen zurückkommen«, kreischte Nataschas Schwester.

Dämmerung.

not agony but a
dullness
suspicion
perfuming evil
supping the
unforgivable and
lonely mediocrity
warmth,compas-
sion, sweetness
burnt feathers

The son devoured all the couscous. He grew tired. He blew out the candle. He crawled between the covers of the bedding.

Midnight.

The wolf entered, "You! We play blind man's bluff."

Silent. Eyes wide open. The son's teeth chattered loudly.

"I hear you. Hold this chime. Run. Or I will catch you," howled the wolf.

The son moaned not a breath. But he could not hide his fear. The chime in his trembling hands echoed loudly.

Daybreak.

Natasha's sister grunted, "Be quick. Bring back my son's reward!" Natasha hurried to the adobe house. Her sister perched by the fence.

Noon.

The mongrel barked, "Bow-wow. Bow-wow. Natasha rides an empty sled, carrying the remains of your son."

"Miserable cur! My boy achieves triumphant success!"

The sister turned around. Natasha handed her a basket. The sister opened the lid. She beheld her son's bones. She began to moan. She flushed red with spite. She dropped dead to the ground.

Natasha and Peter lived happily. Ever after.

Natascha führte den Sohn ihrer Schwester zu dem Kiesstall.

Sonnenuntergang.

Der Sohn hatte alles Stroh zu Gold gesponnen. Er kochte den Hafer. Der schwarze Fuchs erschien und fragte nach einer Hand voll. Der Sohn schrie, »Verschwinde, du böser Geist!«

Der Sohn verschlang den ganzen Kuskus. Er wurde müde. Er blies die Kerze aus. Er kroch zwischen die Decken der Bettstatt.

Mitternacht.

Der Wolf trat ein, »Du! Wir spielen Blindekuh«. Stille. Weit geöffnete Augen. Die Zähne des Sohnes klappterten laut.

»Ich höre dich. Halt dieses Glöckchen. Lauf. Oder ich hole dich«, heulte der Wolf.

Der Sohn hielt den Atem an. Aber er konnte seine Furcht nicht verbergen. Das Glöckchen in seinen zitternden Händen hallte laut wider.

Tagesanbruch.

Nataschas Schwester grinste, »Beeil dich. Bring mir die Belohnung meines Sohnes!« Natascha eilte zu dem Lehmhaus. Ihre Schwester ließ sich am Zaun nieder.

Mittag.

wanting a son
condemned to
greatness
blasts of violent
minds
mingling with
the soil
love and the
marriage ladle
the shrill bird

■

Der Mischling bellte, »Wau-wau. Wau-wau. Natascha lenkt einen leeren Schlitten und führt die Überreste deines Sohnes mit sich«.

»Elendiger Köter! Mein Junge feiert einen triumphalen Sieg!«

Die Schwester drehte sich um. Natascha gab ihr einen Korb. Die Schwester hob den Deckel. Sie erblickte die Gebeine ihres Sohnes. Sie begann zu stöhnen. Sie lief rot an vor Niedertracht. Sie fiel tot um.

Natascha und Peter lebten glücklich. Seitdem.

■

haunted by

shadowy memory

anarchistic

conspiracies of

peace

bigger than nature

captured by the

ineffable

trees to the sky

erasure of the past

Queen of the Jungle /
Königin des Dschungels

resolutely blind
to reality
smell of physical
terror
merging into a
thin haze
drollery floating
magic suffering
fatalist at heart
talking horses

E lephant is very, very, very large. I am sure you will agree when you meet her. Quite stupendous! Indeed gigantic!

Bigger than you. Bigger than me. Bigger than me and you put together. Bigger than the lions. Bigger than the bears. Bigger than the tigers. Bigger than the pears.

Nobody tells her what to do. No how. Elephant is our chieftain. But let's admit it. This crown isn't always so desirable to wear. There are ever so many things to keep track of when you are Queen of the Jungle. You have time to relax only now and again.

It's a tough job.

When Elephant was very young, she was polite and innocent. Naturally curious about the world. She relaxed. She had fun. Just like everybody else.

But as time went by, she grew boastful. She started ordering us around. She believed we couldn't possibly work together. She should control us for our own good. She knew better. Again and again, Leopard and Chimpanzee talked with Elephant, and asked her to be more sensitive to the feelings and dignity of other creatures.

Elephant saw herself as exceptionally understanding, extremely sincere, eternally humble. When she looked into the mirror, she beam-

E lefantin ist sehr, sehr, sehr groß. Ich bin sicher, du wirst mir zustimmen, wenn du sie triffst. Wirklich riesig! Gigantisch gar!

Größer als du. Größer als ich. Größer als du und ich zusammen. Größer als die Löwen. Größer als die Bären. Größer als die Tiger. Größer als die Birnbäume.

Niemand sagt ihr, was sie zu tun hat. Oder wie. Elefantin ist unser Häuptling. Aber das ist in Ordnung. Diese Krone ist nicht immer so leicht zu tragen. Es gibt so unendlich viele Dinge, über die man auf dem Laufenden bleiben muß, wenn man Königin des Dschungels ist. Zeit zu entspannen bleibt dir da nur selten.

Es ist ein harter Job.

Als Elefantin noch sehr jung war, war sie höflich und arglos. Von sich aus neugierig auf die Welt. Sie war entspannt. Sie hatte Spaß. Wie jeder andere auch.

Aber mit der Zeit wurde sie vorlaut. Sie fing an, uns herumzukommandieren. Sie meinte, wir könnten nicht gut zusammenarbeiten. Sie müßte uns zu unserem eigenen Wohl kontrollieren. Sie wußte es besser. Wieder und wieder sprachen Leopard und Schimpanse mit ihr und baten sie, mehr Rücksicht auf die Gefühle und die Würde anderer Geschöpfe zu nehmen.

resembling no
sounds of
language
preferring the
dust
cracked and
crumbling masks
presence
outrunning
apprehension

ed, "I'm the most smartest. I'm the most talented. I'm the most beautiful. I'm the most powerful. I'm the most right. It's someone else's fault when things go wrong!"

We no longer enjoyed her company. We feared telling her the truth. We couldn't talk about the predicament amongst friends. Even in the privacy of our own homes! Someone might inform Elephant, and out of revenge, she would cause lots of trouble.

But one morning, Elephant was intensely, seriously, terribly unkind. She was a big, bumptious, bully. She thought each and every one of us conspired against her.

The families of plants and animals arranged a rendezvous. At Meeting Table, even Beetle chirped up. For the first time ever. She is normally shy. She's oh so small, you see. Her mom and dad are teeny, tiny, too. After digging around for food in the mornings, Beetle spends the rest of the day reading a book by Water Hole. She likes keeping to herself. But she's kind and generous. On Tuesdays and Thursdays, she helps the Younger Ones with their arithmetic.

At Meeting Table that night, Beetle promised to have a heart to heart talk with Elephant. Some giggled as Beetle poured out her feelings. To our surprise, her oration was confident and persuasive. Soon every-

Elefantin sah sich selber als außerordentlich verständig, sehr aufrichtig, unendlich bescheiden. Wenn sie in den Spiegel schaute, strahlte sie, »Ich bin die Klügste. Ich bin die Begabteste. Ich bin die Schönste. Ich bin die Mächtigste. Ich bin immer im Recht. Wenn Dinge schief gehen, ist das jemand anderes Schuld!«

Wir fühlten uns nicht mehr wohl in ihrer Gesellschaft. Wir hatten Angst, ihr die Wahrheit zu sagen. Wir konnten nicht einmal mit unseren Freunden über diese mißliche Lage reden. Auch nicht in unseren eigenen vier Wänden! Jemand hätte Elefantin informieren können. Und aus Rache hätte sie eine Menge Ärger gemacht.

Aber eines Morgens war Elefantin unglaublich, ernsthaft, furchtbar unfreundlich. Sie war eine alberne, aufgeblasene Angeberin. Sie dachte, wir alle hätten uns gegen sie verschworen.

Die Familien der Pflanzen und der Tiere arrangierten ein Treffen. Am Konferenztisch zirpte sogar Käfer auf. Das erste Mal überhaupt. Normalerweise ist sie schüchtern. Sie ist ach so klein, verstehst du. Ihre Mutter und ihr Vater sind auch klitzeklein. Nach dem morgendlichen Rumbuddeln nach Nahrung verbringt Käfer den Rest des Tages mit dem Lesen eines Buches von Wasser Loch. Sie ist gern allein. Aber sie ist freundlich und offen. Dienstags und Donnerstags gibt sie den

difficult struggles
without calm
mute spell of
goodness
deterioration of
intelligence
naked dancing
stars
stunning hail of
powerful attacks

one agreed. She should be allowed this one opportunity. But each and all knew Beetle may not come back alive, and we were apprehensive.

Elephant didn't learn of the discussion. She snorted, "What nonsense! Who can take Beetle seriously? She is little—an itty bitty, peewee, runt! She is not as important as I."

On Friday afternoon, while Elephant lay sunning in the grass, asleep after a delicious lunch, Beetle crawled into her ear. A few minutes later Elephant woke up with a scream of pain—Beetle was scampering about her ear canal.

Elephant went on a rampage! She knocked down the Palm Trees —and they didn't like that. She rolled around the dirt and crushed the Termites—and they didn't like that. She jumped up and down on the Lawn Chair Furniture set up for Giraffe's birthday party—and he didn't like that. And neither did the Lawn Chair Furniture for that matter!

Elephant seemed bent on destroying all in her path. But Beetle didn't go away. She stayed put. As snug as a bug in Elephant's ear.

Elephant couldn't catch a wink of sleep. She missed her second, third and fourth midafternoon siestas. Round midnight, she begged Beetle to show some mercy.

Beetle replied, "I will crawl out of your ear if you do us this favor.

Jüngeren Nachhilfe in Rechnen.

Am Konferenztisch an jenem Abend versprach Käfer, sich ein Herz zu nehmen und mit Elefantin zu sprechen. Einige kicherten, als Käfer ihren Gefühlen freien Lauf ließ. Zu unser aller Überraschung war ihre Rede zuversichtlich und überzeugend. Schnell stimmten alle zu. Sie sollte diese eine Chance bekommen. Aber jeder wußte, daß Käfer vielleicht nicht lebend zurückkommen würde, und das machte uns Sorgen.

Elefantin lernte nicht aus der Unterredung. Sie schnaubte, »Was für ein Unsinn! Wer kann Käfer schon ernst nehmen? Sie ist klein – ein itzi-bitzi Wurzelzwerg. Sie ist nicht so bedeutend wie ich.«

Am Freitag Nachmittag, während Elefantin sich im Gras sonnte, schläfrig von einem köstlichen Mal, krabbelte Käfer in ihr Ohr. Wenige Minuten später erwachte Elefantin mit einem Schmerzensschrei: Käfer tollte in ihrem Ohrkanal herum.

Elefantin drehte durch! Sie riß die Palmen um – und die mochten das nicht. Sie wälzte sich auf dem Boden und zermalmte die Termiten – und die mochten das nicht. Sie trampelte auf den Gartenmöbeln herum, die für Giraffes Geburtstagsparty bereitstanden – und der mochte das nicht. Und genauso wenig hielten die Gartenmöbel davon!

Elefantin schien alles, was ihr in den Weg kam, zerstören zu müs-

vomiting black
blood
loved most dearly
of all
suffering with
the mortals
hearts of the good
praying to avenge
the hearth
the dark pain

Tomorrow you must talk with all the Plants and Animals, the Stones and Minerals, the Bacteria and Viruses. You must ask them to forgive you for your selfish behavior. They will understand all of your pressures, all of your worries. You must listen to our suggestions on how to live together in a more affectionate and benevolent way."

Laying beside Riverbank that evening, Elephant tossed and turned. She reflected on the path her life had taken. She realized the arrogance of her actions.

In the morning, Elephant gathered everyone around her for a talk. We conversed all day long, and by dusk we came to a new understanding and appreciation for each other. Elephant agreed to continue as our Queen. Everyone cheered. We lifted her on our shoulders, and threw her into Big Pond. Goldfish gave her a wonderful massage. Afterwards, she dined on Porcelain, accompanied by Silverware.

Elephant slept marvelously that night. Tranquil and cheery. The following afternoon she presented constructive ideas on how everyone could live together in a much, much happier way.

And for awhile we all turned out to be very pleased indeed...

sen. Aber Käfer ging nicht raus. Sie blieb wie festgewachsen. Das Ganze wie eine Wanze in Elefantins Ohr.

Elefantin konnte kein Auge zutun. Sie verpaßte ihre zweite, dritte und vierte Nachmittagssiesta. Gegen Mitternacht flehte sie Käfer um Gnade an.

Käfer antwortete, »Ich werde aus deinem Ohr rauskrabbeln, wenn du uns einen Gefallen tust. Morgen mußt du mit allen Pflanzen und Tieren, den Steinen und Mineralien, den Bakterien und Viren reden. Du mußt sie um Verzeihung bitten für dein selbstsüchtiges Benehmen. Sie werden Verständnis haben für all deine Nöte, all deine Sorgen. Du mußt dir unsere Vorschläge anhören, wie wir in herzlicher und inniger Weise zusammenleben können«.

An Flußufer liegend, warf sich Elefantin an diesem Abend unruhig hin und her. Sie dachte nach über den Lauf, den ihr Leben genommen hatte. Ihr wurde die Arroganz ihres Handelns bewußt.

Am Morgen versammelte Elefantin alle zum Gespräch um sich. Wir redeten den ganzen Tag miteinander, und bei Einbruch der Dämmerung hatten wir zu einem neuen Verständnis und neuer Wertschätzung füreinander gefunden. Elefantin war einverstanden, unsere Königin zu bleiben. Alle jubelten. Wir hoben sie auf unsere Schultern

strife and tumult
and death
glorious lame sex
the divine boar
maidens in
churlish glee
cutting the throat
with a pitiless knife
belly of the whale
delicious mead

■

und warfen sie in den Großen Teich. Goldfisch gab ihr eine wunderbare Massage. Später dinierte sie mit Porzellan und Tafelsilber.

Diese Nacht schlief Elefantin traumhaft. Ruhig und süß. Am folgenden Nachmittag präsentierte sie konstruktive Pläne, wie alle viel, viel glücklicher zusammenleben könnten.

Und eine Zeitlang waren wir auch alle wirklich zufrieden...

■

everything going
right
warbling robust
pleasure
kinship of genius
fairy rulers
upholding the
heavens
women spinning
the wheel

Brothers and Sisters/
Brüder und Schwestern

predilection for
eccentricity
fallacious
banalities of the
perfect
vagabond from
the soul
climbing into the
source
disregarding hope

Days of grace. Flowers bloomed year round. Children walked strong and aristocratic. Families lived in tranquillity. The Clan fought no Enemy. Pleasure enveloped the Mountain.

In this land of enchantment, the most marvelous of the marvelous palaces was that of Brother and Rose. The couple veritably gifted. The household truly kind. Anything Bad passing through the charmed portals of their nuptial castle was transformed into the Good.

Brother was the son of Queen and King. Sister his double. She emerged from the cosmos at the same moment. She appeared identical. Identical in every shape and limb, save one. Sister was without eyes.

Sister inhabited a lavish château with her six children. She taught the Clan the secrets of the herbs. For although she was blind, she knew the smell and taste of each thing living on the Mountain.

Every evening Brother and Sister made love in the garden of their parents' estate, the pale starlight undulating. Afterwards they strolled amongst the flowering perfumed groves. Brother striding proud and talking garrulous. Sister walking side by side, rib by rib. Listening intently.

Brother could interpret the carvings on the ancient tower placed in the center of his courtyard. This alchemical writing had been passed

Tage der Gnade. Blumen blühten das ganze Jahr. Kinder wandelten gesund und aufrecht. Die Familien lebten in Frieden. Der Clan hatte keine Feinde. Zufriedenheit umhüllte den Berg.

In diesem verzauberten Land war der wunderbarste aller wunderbaren Paläste der von Bruder und Rose. Ein wahrlich beneidenswertes Paar. Ihr Haushalt wirklich liebenswürdig. Alles Schlechte, das die bezaubernden Tore ihres ehelichen Schlosses passierte, wurde in Gutes verwandelt.

Bruder war der Sohn von Königin und König. Schwester sein Ebenbild. Sie war dem Kosmos zur selben Zeit entsprungen. Sie war identisch. Identisch in jeder Form und jedem Glied, außer in einem. Schwester hatte keine Augen.

Schwester bewohnte mit ihren sechs Kindern ein weitläufiges Château. Sie lehrte den Clan die Geheimnisse der Kräuter. Denn obwohl sie blind war, kannte sie Geruch und Gestalt jedes lebenden Dinges auf dem Berg.

Jeden Abend liebten sich Bruder und Schwester im Garten ihrer Eltern, umwoben vom blassen Licht der Sterne. Anschließend schlenderten sie in den blühend duftenden Hainen. Bruder stolz schreitend und offenherzig redend. Schwester mit ihm Seite an Seite, Rippe an

arousal of
blankness
gnawing at bones
stinking gratitude
bewildering
shapes and forms
incarnating the
snow-white
serpent
bewitched genie

to the Clan by an unknown tribe, long forgotten. With these hieroglyphs, Brother could peer into the future of others. But not of his own.

In the spring of that year. Turning solemn. Remaining austere. Brother no longer danced at the festivals celebrating rebirth. He kept to himself, taking long rides into the forest. But he did not understand why he chose a solitary life.

In consternation, King and Queen assembled all the leaders at the table round. Querying Brother, "Name the birthplace of your confusion. Where vanished your indissoluble confidence?"

"Evil prowls intimately beside me as I sleep to dream," Brother whispered. "I smell Death. I'm frozen as if a statue, strangled by a power greater than I. When I awake the mien of my assassin vanishes from memory."

From the cryptic soothsayer, Queen learned of Brother's fate. She had not permitted herself to inquire before. Hoping to change destiny, Queen saddled her griffin. After three nights of riding on arduous terrain. After abstaining from all food and drink while undertaking her pilgrimage. After taking a vow of silence. Queen made her way to The Divide, marking the Southern boundary of Death's territory.

Queen rode through Barren Forest, until she came to the Gates of

Rippe. Innig lauschend.

Bruder konnte die eingemeißelten Zeichen auf dem alten Turm in der Mitte seines Hofes deuten. Diese alchemistischen Formeln waren dem Clan von einem unbekannten, längst vergessenen Stamm vermacht worden. Mit Hilfe dieser Hieroglyphen konnte Bruder in die Zukunft anderer spähen. Aber nicht in seine eigene.

Im Frühling dieses Jahres. Wurde er ernst. Blieb er abweisend. Bruder tanzte nicht länger zu den Festen der Wiedergeburt. Er blieb in sich gekehrt, unternahm lange Ausritte in den Wald. Aber er verstand nicht, warum er sich zurückzog.

Bestürzt versammelten Königin und König all ihre Berater um den runden Tisch. Bruder befragend, »Nenn uns den Geburtsort deiner Verwirrung. Wohin floh deine unerschöpfliche Zuversicht?«

»Böses umschleicht mich ahnungsvoll, sobald ich zu träumen beginne«, flüsterte Bruder. »Ich rieche Tod. Ich bin starr wie eine Statue, eingeschnürt von einer Kraft, die größer ist als ich. Wenn ich aufwache, verschwindet die Fratze meines Meuchlers aus der Erinnerung.«

Von dem geheimnisvollen Wahrsager erfuhr Königin Bruders Schicksal. Sie hatte sich vorher nicht getraut nachzuforschen. In der Hoffnung, das Schicksal abzuwenden, sattelte Königin ihren Greif.

pack of rabid dogs
reverence in the
sun
childish scruples
of the heart
sane meaning,
mad outcome
forlorn under the
blue sky
poison tattletale

the Underworld. Guarding the entrance, Death's enormous Hydra growled fiercely: opposing those of the Living who wished to enter the realm of the Eternal Dead.

The Hydra ordered, "Who rides upon Queen's stallion?" Queen replied, disguised as an old woman, "I am called the Hag."

"Advance, Hag," commanded the Hydra.

Queen did not seek Death's citadel. Instead she strode to the small clandestine tomb where the Inquisitor lay buried. Kneeling above its grave, Queen mixed her own blood with the soil, reciting the hymn of the lullaby she sang Brother and Sister to sleep each night. The ground began to bubble and churn. The Inquisitor emerged. Its gaunt face withered. Its bloated body pockmarked.

The Inquisitor moaned, "Entombed by rotting earth. Soaked by foul rain. Fed upon by vermin. Why have I been awakened after an eternity?"

"I seek knowledge from the Underworld," trembled Queen. "Why are Death's workers merrily spreading the Great Room's tables with elixirs of ambrosia? Why are the cloisonné heralds so majestically displayed?"

"Death fashions a glorious welcome for Brother," intoned the Inquisitor. "Do not ask me to break my vow of silence again."

Nach dreinächtigem Ritt durch unwegsames Gelände. Nach Enthaltsamkeit von jedwedem Essen und Trinken während ihrer Pilgerschaft. Nach Ablegen eines Schweigegelübdes. Gelangte Königin zu der Scheidelinie, die die südliche Grenze des Territoriums von Tod markierte.

Königin ritt durch Dürren Forst, bis sie zu den Toren der Unterwelt kam. Vor dem Eingang knurrte Tods riesige Hydra grimmig: sich denjenigen Lebenden in den Weg stellend, die das Reich des Ewigen Todes betreten wollten.

Die Hydra fragte knapp, »Wer reitet auf dem königlichen Hengst?« Königin, als alte Frau verkleidet, antwortete, »Ich werde die Greisin genannt«.

»Geh weiter, Greisin«, kommandierte die Hydra.

Königin aber ging nicht zur Hofburg des Todes. Stattdessen eilte sie zu dem verborgenen Grab, in dem der Inquisitor begraben lag. Über sein Grab gebeugt, mischte Königin ihr Blut mit Erde und summte dabei die Melodie des Schlafliedes, das sie Bruder und Schwester jeden Abend zum Einschlafen gesungen hatte. Der Boden begann zu blubbern und zu schäumen. Der Inquisitor erschien. Sein hageres Gesicht eingefallen. Sein aufgequollener Leib voller Narben.

Der Inquisitor ächzte, »Begraben in verrottender Erde. Aufgeweicht

rumor of
struggling mutiny
bodies of absurd
deportment
descending
amiably into love
never at a loss
thread of fate
twisting
returning home

"One last time!" pleaded Queen. "When all mourn Brother, who alone remains smiling?"

"It is obvious you seek the perpetrator, Hag, if that be your true name. Perhaps you may postpone Brother's karma for a brief measure of time," sneered the Inquisitor. "But you cannot change the course of the seasons."

Suddenly, thousands of worms attacked the body of the Inquisitor, turning the grave into a mound of putrid foaming soil. And for a moment the Hydra ceased baying.

Queen mounted her griffin, and with profound desolation, flew quickly back to the Clan. When arriving at the entrance of her home, Queen beheld her King in the Dome of the Sky, his temperament cheerful.

"Brother cannot die!" he rang out. "I have obliged the Mountain in a treaty of peace! Each and all make a promise! Between the Stones and the Alloys. Between the Minerals and the Dirt. Between the Organisms of the Ether and the Things of the Sea. The Earth, the Wind, the Fire give their word. The Killing Venoms and Wasting Diseases—they too pledge no hurt!"

Queen smiled bitterly. For while Brother's demise would not take

von faulem Regen. Genährt von Würmern. Warum wurde ich nach einer Ewigkeit geweckt?«

»Ich suche Rat aus der Unterwelt«, zitterte Königin. »Warum decken Todes Arbeiter so freudig die Tische mit Trünken aus Ambrosia? Warum sind die Cloisonné-Wappen so majestätisch herausgeputzt?«

»Tod bereitet Bruder einen triumphalen Empfang«, tönte der Inquisitor. »Zwing mich nicht noch einmal, mein Schweigegelübde zu brechen.«

»Eine letzte Frage!« flehte Königin. »Wenn alle um Bruder trauern, wer allein lacht dann noch?«

»Es ist offensichtlich, daß du den Frevler suchst, Greisin, wenn das denn dein wahrer Name ist. Vielleicht kannst du Bruders Karma für eine kurze Zeit aufschieben«, höhnte der Inquisitor. »Aber du kannst nicht den Wandel der Jahreszeiten aufhalten.«

Plötzlich attackierten tausende Würmer den Körper des Inquisitors und verwandelten das Grab in einen Haufen modrig schäumender Erde. Und für einen Moment hörte die Hydra auf zu bellen.

Königin bestieg ihren Greif und flog in tiefem Gram schnell zurück zu ihrem Clan. Als sie am Eingangstor ihres Hauses ankam, erblickte sie ihren König gut gelaunt am Firmament.

»Bruder kann nicht sterben!« brachte er hervor. »Ich habe den Berg

fatal coincidence
of vanished youth
robbers voyaging
about
father buried in
the mud
monstrous
swollen waves
no help for the
weeping

place forthwith, she understood kismet would someday find a new means of ending Brother's life.

Everything changed.

All the Clan quickly learned of the covenant. Amidst an era of frolic. Because of a surfeit of leisure. A new tournament was organized to occupy their time.

Swinging a sword with her fierce grip as if to hew Brother into sections, Iron marveled how her sharp blade bent like rubber, and Brother remained unblemished.

Countless times Bronze threw his magic boomerang. This weapon which had massacred the Enemy time and again, returned to his left claw without ruffling a hair on Brother's neck.

Silver catapulted thousands of rocks with its slingshot. The sharp stones bounced harmlessly away as if Brother wore invisible armor.

Ignored, Realist lurked amidst this crowd of happy Clan folk. Brother no longer valued his counsel. For now Idealist towered as his only favorite. Realist's ardent love for Brother smoldered into hatred.

Surrounded by an assembly that disavowed evil, Realist sought revenge. Not even the Depraved Ghost, nor the Bloodthirsty Monster wanted to harm Brother. Not the Spider in the Woodshed. Not the

zu einem Friedensvertrag gezwungen! Jeder einzelne gibt sein Wort. Von den Steinen zu den Metallen. Von den Mineralien zum Staub. Von den Organismen des Äthers zu den Bewohnern des Meeres. Die Erde, der Wind, das Feuer geben ihr Wort. Die tödlichen Gifte und die verheerenden Krankheiten – auch sie geloben Verschonung!«

Königin lächelte bitter. Eine Zeitlang würde Bruders Ableben aufgeschoben sein. Sie wußte, daß das Kismet eines Tages einen neuen Weg finden würde, Bruders Leben zu beenden.

Alles änderte sich.

Der ganze Clan lernte schnell aus dem Vertrag. Es folgte eine Zeit der Ausgelassenheit. Wegen eines Übermaßes an Muße. Ein neues Turnier wurde organisiert, um ihnen die Zeit zu vertreiben.

Ein Schwert mit ihrem festen Griff schwingend, wie um Bruder in Stücke zu schlagen, staunte Eisen nicht schlecht, als ihre scharfe Klinge sich wie Gummi bog, und Bruder unversehrt blieb.

Unzählige Male warf Bronze seinen magischen Bumerang. Diese Waffe, die ein ums andere Mal den Gegner bezwungen, kehrte nun in seine linke Pranke zurück, ohne Bruder ein Haar gekrümmt zu haben.

Silber schleuderte tausende Steinbrocken mit seinem Katapult. Die spitzen Steine prallten wirkungslos ab, als ob Bruder eine unsichtbare

living the
nameless whim
empty look of
spiteful mystery
strongest and full
of confidence
brooding space of
a sister
mistrust of the
domineering

Crocodile in the River. Unhinged by hate, Realist began to scheme.

In the cold morning, while King sat weaving clouds in the Dome of the Sky, there came a young boy.

"The voices of gaiety drift by me. What forms this rapture?" King asked the callow lad.

"I don't understand," he stuttered. "They practice a magic rite. Brother poses calm and smiling. Then the Clan toss sticks and stones to break his bones. But he never comes tumbling down."

"'Tis no puzzle," exclaimed King. "All things pledge to guard Brother against harm!"

"Have each and every one of the Branches and Bushes, Mushrooms and Molds, Plankton and Papyrus agreed?" persisted the child.

"Of course," nodded King.

"East of our Mountain, presides Oak," explained the juvenile. "From it emerges Mistletoe. This demure spot of green does not spring directly from the ground. Does Mistletoe promise no damage?"

"The darling of the Celtic people? I never understood why they use it for their rituals. To me it behaves subservient. Appears delicate. My conviction is that it cannot wound," announced King. "So I did not disorder its slumber."

Rüstung trüge.

Unbeachtet lungerte Realist inmitten dieser glücklichen Schar. Bruder schätze seinen Rat nicht mehr. Im Moment ragte nur Idealist als sein einziger Favorit heraus. Realists glühende Zuneigung für Bruder gefror zu Haß.

Umzingelt von Leuten, die das Böse leugnen, sann Realist auf Rache. Nicht einmal der Verdorbene Geist, noch das Blutrünstige Monster wollten Bruder übel mitspielen. Nicht die Spinne im Holzschuppen. Nicht das Krokodil im Fluß. Zerfressen von Haß, begann Realist Ränke zu schmieden.

Eines kalten Morgens, als König wolkenwebend am Firmament saß, kam ein Junge des Weges.

»Die Stimme des Frohsinns ist mir zugeflogen. Woher deine Begeisterung?«, fragte König den unreifen Burschen.

»Ich weiß nicht«, stotterte dieser. »Sie üben ein magisches Ritual aus. Bruder zeigt sich ruhig und lächelnd. Dann schleudert der Clan Stöcke und Steine, um ihm die Knochen zu brechen. Aber er stürzt nicht einmal nieder.«

»'s ist kein Wunder«, rief König aus. »Alle Dinge gelobten, Bruder vor Übel zu schützen!«

spirit bedded to a
morality
changing form at
will
bones foaming up
the hills
scattering brains
upon the horizon
precious beyond
compare

"A creature suckling from Oak," assured the infant. "This parasite need engender no distrust."

The boy clasped together both his hands in thankful prayer, then skipped onward. King crouched forward to continue his task of weaving. Yet a discomfort gripped him, and he could not easily dismiss it.

Outside the Dome of the Sky, Realist the One Without Love, returned to the shape of his true self, and rushed to Oak. He spoke to Mistletoe in its own language—pretending to be of assistance. As soon as Mistletoe relaxed its grip, he snipped it away from the tree. Realist shaped the innocent plant into the form of an Arrow. Kissing Mistletoe, he muttered a curse, transforming the pliant stem into steel. Hiding the Arrow, Realist returned to the tournament site.

Reveling in jocular assembly, the Clan invented new rules for their grand sport. Now the contest was to see how cleverly and with what style the impotent weapons could be tossed. A panel of judges, selected with an eye towards neutrality, ranked the contestants. The Scribe noted the scores in his gold leafed ledger. Opening gambits and end game strategies were published and discussed late into the night.

A family of Bears, who had petitioned for an opportunity to participate in the games, threw malicious words at Brother. These splin-

»Hat jeder einzelne Baum und Busch, Moder und Moos, Plankton und Papyrus zugstimmt?«, beharrte das Kind.

»Natürlich«, nickte der König.

»Östlich unseres Berges thront Eiche«, erklärte der Jüngling. »An ihr klettert Mistel empor. Dieses spröde Grünzeug wächst nicht direkt aus dem Boden. Hat Mistel versprochen, keinen Schaden anzurichten?«

»Der Liebling der Kelten? Ich habe nie verstanden, warum sie es für ihre Rituale benutzten. Für mich benimmt es sich parasitär. Anscheinend delikat. Nach meiner Überzeugung kann es nicht schaden«, verkündete der König. »Also habe ich seinen Schlummer nicht gestört.«

»Ein von Eiche bemuttertes Geschöpf«, versicherte das Kind. »Diesem Parasiten muß man kein Mißtrauen entgegenbringen.«

Der Junge faltete dankbar seine Hände wie zum Gebet und sprang von dannen. König beugte sich wieder nach vorn, um mit dem Weben fortzufahren. Trotzdem ergriff ihn ein Unbehagen, das er nicht so einfach wieder los wurde.

Außerhalb des Firmaments kehrte Realist, Der-Eine-ohne-Liebe, zurück zu seiner wahren Gestalt und eilte zu Eiche. Er sprach zu Mistel in ihrer Sprache – angeblich, um ihr zu helfen. Aber sobald Mistel ihre Umklammerung lockerte, riß er sie vom Baum ab. Realist formte aus

waiting for the
release of night
beautiful virgins
always coming
back to life again
small bite of
magic fruit
make anew and
youthful
the found dread

tered into polished nuggets when hitting their target. The Ten Headed Wolves spewing bolts of fire, joined the festivities too.

Amidst all the excitement and glee, Sister remained aloof from this exorcism. Each afternoon she reclined on a stone bench a short distance away. Lost in her own world while knitting a pair of trousers for one of her offspring.

"Why are you not playing?" posed Realist, appearing suddenly next to her.

"Invisible am I. Signaling no affection by hurtling a stone," cried Sister.

"Tell me the source of your frustration," murmured Realist.

"Since the call of romance has ended. I will confess our intimacy," breathed Sister. "He no longer craves me. An abundance of secret lovers will be his for eternity."

"I reveal my lust for Brother too," confirmed Realist. "But I have consulted the Oracle, and return with a remedy for our despair. In my palm rests an Arrow, fashioned by Eros, made for you alone. Love will enter Brother's body and transform him into the one who covets you."

"And you?" queried Sister.

"My shaft follows," smiled Realist.

der unschuldigen Pflanze einen Pfeil. Während er Mistel küßte, murmelte er eine Verwünschung und verwandelte den biegsamen Zweig zu Stahl. Den Pfeil verborgen, kehrte Realist zurück zum Tunierplatz.

Sich an heiterem Beisammensein ergötzend, erfand der Clan immer neue Regeln für seinen großartigen Sport. Jetzt ging der Wettbewerb darum, zu sehen, wie gescheit und in welchem Stil die unwirksamen Waffen geschleudert werden konnten. Ein neutrales Schiedsgericht legte die Reihenfolge der Teilnehmer fest. Der Schreiber notierte die Treffer in seinem goldbeschlagenen Buch. Eröffnungszüge und Endspielstrategien wurden veröffentlicht und bis spät in die Nacht diskutiert.

Eine Bärenfamilie, die um die Erlaubnis an den Spielen teilzunehmen gebeten hatte, warf mit gehässigen Worten nach Bruder. Sie zersplitterten zu polierten Klumpen, sobald sie ihr Ziel trafen. Selbst die Zehnköpfigen Wölfe nahmen feuerspeiend an den Festlichkeiten teil.

Inmitten der ganzen Aufregung und Heiterkeit, blieb Schwester abseits dieser Exorzismen. Jeden Nachmittag ruhte sie sich auf einer Steinbank in einiger Entfernung aus. Gedankenverloren in ihrer eigenen Welt, während sie ein paar Hosen für ihren Nachwuchs strickte.

»Warum spielst du nicht mit?«, posierte Realist, plötzlich neben ihr auftauchend.

remembrance of
courage
admonition of
silence
the pagan dragon
bleeding
deserted and
useless looking
extinguishing
the fire

Realist placed the Mistletoe Arrow in Sister's hand. Sister threw the missile with all the force of her desire. The Arrow entered freely into the heart of the esteemed champion.

Brother collapsed. His breath of life extinguished forever.

■

»Unsichtbar bin ich. Indem ich einen Stein werfe, zeige ich keine Gemütsregung«, schluchzte Schwester.

»Nenn mir den Grund deiner Enttäuschung«, murmelte Realist.

»Der Ruf der Liebe ist zu Ende gegangen. Ich gestehe unsere Innigkeit ein«, hauchte Schwester. »Er sehnt sich nicht mehr nach mir. Ein Sturm an heimlichen Verehrern wird ihn bis in alle Ewigkeit verfolgen.«

»Auch ich gestehe meine Lust auf Bruder«, bestätigte Realist. »Aber ich habe das Orakel befragt und kehre zurück mit einem Mittel gegen unsere Verzweiflung. In meiner Hand ruht ein Pfeil, angefertigt von Eros, allein für dich gemacht. Liebe wird in Bruders Körper eindringen und ihn in denjenigen verwandeln, der dich begehrt.«

»Und du?«, zweifelte Schwester.

»Mein Pfeil folgt«, grinste Realist.

Realist legte den Mistelpfeil in Schwesters Hand. Schwester schleuderte die Spitze mit der ganzen Kraft ihrer Sehnsucht. Der Pfeil drang ohne Widerstand in das Herz des gefeierten Helden.

Bruder brach zusammen. Sein Lebenshauch erlosch auf ewig.

■

one of the
immortals
spray from a
pungent flower
jackal-snapping
lies
blossoming vision
opulent webs
seducing
honking geese

Birth of a Poet /
Geburt eines Dichters

redeeming facts
of innocence
exalted howling
creatures
growing greedy
about the mouth
fire burning out
of control
anchor of blood
quickly drying

I was lollygaggin' with me mum, me dad and me younger sis. We had traveled our journey a good ways, and then some. The sun glowed molten red. Made a person feel downright thirsty it did. We sat by the sycamore tree. Indeed we was tired.

We snoozed till dusk. By then me throat was parched. I spied a well. I ain't seen it before. I called to me sis, "Lend a hand! Bring some balm here for us good folk." She moseyed to the well. Bent her waist over the rim to grab the bucket, when holy smokes, she's clutchin' her eye, hollerin' agony.

Me mum burst over to gauge the matter. She peeked down the hole, wonderin' why me sis hadn't brang the water. Sure enough her ocular fell out the same like.

Me dad's a meddlesome one he is. He dittoed them. Walked hisself over to gander the fussin' and cussin'. Peerin' down steady. Off fell his lenticular.

I must admit. I was no different than the rest. I sashayed to the spot and me pupil plummeted into the fathomless pit.

To size up our predicament—one, two, three, four. Four eyes at the bottom of the cistern.

We was a moanin' and a groanin', when a fellow traveler passed

Ich war am faulenzen mit meiner Ma, meim Pa und meiner kleinen Schwester. Auf unserm Weg warn wir 'n gutes Stück und 'n bißchen vorangekommen. Die Sonne gluhte feuerrot. Machte einen sofort total durstig. Wir saßen unterm Ahornbaum. Mann, waren wir müde.

Wir schnarchten bis es dämmerte. Dann war meine Kehle völlig ausgetrocknet. Ich ortete einen Brunnen. Hatte ihn vorher nicht gesehen. Ich rief meine Schwester, »Tu mir 'n Gefallen! Bring uns was Flüssiges.« Sie trottete zum Brunnen. Beugte ihren Oberkörper übern Rand, um den Eimer zu packen, als auf einmal, hoppla, sie nach ihrem Auge schnappte, heiliger Strohsack.

Meine Ma rannte rüber, um die Lage zu peilen. Blinzelte runter in das Loch, verdutzt, warum meine Schwester das Wasser nicht gebracht hat. Klare Sache, daß ihr das Okular auf dieselbe Weise rausfiel.

Mein Pa ist auch so'n Schlauer. Machte es ihnen nach. Bewegte sich rüber, um nach dem Getue und Gefluche zu schaun. Glotzte stracks runter. Und raus fiel sein Guckerchen.

Ich muß sagen. Ich war nicht besser als der Rest. Schlenderte zu der Stelle, und schon plumpste meine Pupille in den bodenlosen Schacht.

Um unsere mißliche Lage mal darzulegen: Eins, zwei, drei, vier.

whirring
commotion of
thoughts
preternatural
giddiness
mercy of salacious
phantoms
fetal contours of
spurious logic
riddle of the wolf

by. He stopped for a giggle and a goggle. Askin' about our misery. We four told him the whole story we did.

The traveler said, "I'll tell you what. I'll jump down that cavern, and fetch them lenses. Cause what's happened to you is this—the well goblin done snatched away your corneas. When I gets back up, the bargain is I keeps two of 'em. What d'ya say?"

"Fair enough stranger," wailed I. And the rest of the bunch nodded their noggins.

Down he went. In a blink he bounced back up, all four optics in the palm of his left hand. He pocketed the two. "Good luck to yer all," grinned he with a hoot, scamperin' off.

What were we to do?

I took a knife, n' cut out me dad's other eye. Then it all divided up even like. One for me, one for me mum and one for me sis.

■

Vier Augen auf'm Grund der Zisterne.

Wir am Jaulen und am Maulen, als ein Mitreisender vorbeikam. Hielt an um zu Glotzen und zu Frotzeln. Fragte nach unserm Pech. Wir vier haben ihm dann die ganze Geschichte erzählt.

Der Reisende sagte, »Ich schlag' euch was vor. Ich spring' in diese Höhle und hol' diese Linsen. Weil, was euch passiert ist, ist folgendes: der Brunnenkobold hat euch eure Hornhäute weggeschnappt. Falls ich wieder hochkomme, darf ich zur Belohnung zwei davon behalten. Wie findet ihr das?«

»Fair genug, Fremder«, wimmerte ich. Und der Rest der Truppe nickte mit den Nasen.

Runter ging's mit ihm. Im selben Augenblick federte er wieder hoch, alle vier Optiken in seiner linken Hand. Zwei kassierte er direkt ein. »Viel Glück euch«, grinste er mit Gehupe und düste davon.

Was sollten wir schon machen?

Ich hab' ein Messer genommen und das andere Auge meines Vaters 'rausgeschnitten. Damit es auch alles genau auskam. Eins für mich, eins für meine Ma und eins für meine Schwester.

■

Acknowledgment

This book is the weave of phrases on the left, with stories on the right. These phrases are inspired by the fairy tales of history, religion, literature, biography and the like. Sources for the stories:

The Tale of...

1) *One Thousand Nights and a Night* 2) Mary Shelley and friends telling ghost stories at their villa near Lake Geneva. 3) The Titanic. Each of the fairy tales in my book is told by a different character. But after the first, I leave it up to you to group together who tells what story.

The Struggle of I

My retelling of the myth of Athena and Arachne. 1) Ovid's *Metamorphoses*, translated by Mary M. Innes. Published by Penguin Books, London. Copyright © 1955 Patricia Terry. 2) *Bulfinch's Mythology, The Age of Fable, The Age of Chivalry, The Legends of Charlemagne*, by Thomas Bulfinch. Published by Modern Library Edition. Biographical note Copyright © 1993 Random House Inc.

Return of the Garden

1) The kernel of this story: "The Grateful Snake" from *Indian Tales*, by Romila Thapar. First published by Penguin Books India (P) Ltd., now a Puffin Book, reprinted 1992. Copyright © 1991 Romila Thapar. In "The Grateful Snake," it's a girl who meets her prince charming. I reverse the gender of the main characters and plot ambiguity about who owns whom. I also leave the ending, and sexual relations undetermined. 2) Influential: "He saved a snake and won a wife, slapped his wife and lost his life" from *Mayan Tales from Zinacantan: Dreams and Stories from the People of the Bat*, collected and translated by Robert M. Laughlin. Edited by Carol Karasik. Published by the Smithsonian Institution Press, Washington and London. Copyright © 1988 Carol Karasik. 3) Besides my reading of Indian folklore: Aesop's "Androcles and the Lion", about an escaped slave who rescues a lion, and is rewarded for his selfless deed: from *Aesop's Fables. Literally Translated from the Greek*, by Geo. Fyler Townsend. Published by The American News Company, New York. (No date for this book, maybe late 1890's. It's my maternal grandmother's copy.) It has been said that Aesop borrows from ancient Indian folktales, long before him. 4) For cross-cultural variations of an individual swallowing a needy snake, I looked to African folklore. In one Hausa version it is in the form of a dilemma. The moral of the story is induced by posing the negative—the snake is not grateful for being saved, and things go wrong. See for example "Ingratitude" in *Yes and No: The Intimate Folklore of Africa*, by Alta Jablow. A Greenwood Press, Publishers reprinting 1973; Westport, Connecticut. Originally published in 1961 by Horizon Press, New York. Copyright © 1961 Alta Jablow. In this vein, Aesop gives us "The Farmer and the Snake".

The Gift

This is my retelling of a Native American story involving Coyote, Iktome, Fox or combinations of the two. 1) From the White River Sioux, "Coyote, Iktome and The Rock" from *American Indian Myths and Legends*, selected and edited by Richard Erdoes and Alfonso Ortiz. Published by Pantheon Books, New York; a division of

Anmerkungen

Dieses Buch ist ein Gewebe aus Phrasen auf der linken Seite und Geschichten auf der rechten. Die Phrasen sind inspiriert von bekannten Märchen, Religion, Literatur, Biographien und ähnlichem. Quellen für die Geschichten waren:

Die Erzählung von...

1) *Tausendundeine Nacht* 2) Mary Shelley und ihre Freunde, wie sie in ihrer Villa nahe des Genfer Sees Gespenstergeschichten erzählen. 3) Die Titanic. Jedes Märchen hier wird von einer anderen Person erzählt. Aber nach dem ersten überlasse ich es dem Leser, herauszufinden, wer welche Geschichte erzählt.

Der Kampf des Ich

Meine Nacherzählung des Mythos von Athene und Arachne. 1) Ovids *Metamorphosen*, ins Engl. übersetzt von Mary M. Innes. Penguin Books, London. Copyright © 1955 Patricia Terry. 2) *Bulfinch's Mythology, The Age of Fable, The Age of Chivalry, The Legends of Charlemagne*, von Thomas Bulfinch. Modern Library Edition. Copyright © 1993 Random House Inc.

Rückkehr des Gartens

1) Der Kern der Geschichte: *The Grateful Snake* aus *Indian Tales*, von Romila Thapar. Zuerst veröffentlicht von Penguin Books India (P) Ltd., jetzt ein Puffin Book, wiederveröffentlicht 1992. Copyright © 1991 Romila Thapar. In *The Grateful Snake* ist es ein Mädchen, das ihren Prinzen trifft. Ich vertausche die Geschlechter der Figuren und die Zweideutigkeit der Handlung, wer wen besitzt. Ich lasse auch das Ende und die sexuellen Beziehungen unbestimmt. 2) Beeinflußt von: *He saved a snake and won a wife, slapped his wife and lost his life* in *Mayan Tales from Zinacantan: Dreams and Stories from the People of the Bat*, zusammengestellt und ins Engl. übersetzt von Robert M. Laughlin. Hg. von Carol Karasik. Smithsonian Institution Press, Washington und London. Copyright © 1988 Carol Karasik. 3) Neben meiner Beschäftigung mit indischen Sagen: Aesops *Androkles und der Löwe* über einen entflohenen Sklaven, der einen Löwen rettet und für seine selbstlose Tat belohnt wird: aus *Aesop's Fables. Literally Translated from the Greek*, von Geo. Fyler Townsend, The American News Company, New York (o.J., Ende 19. Jh. Die Ausgabe ist von meiner Großmutter mütterlicherseits). Es ist bekannt, daß Aesop selber von alten indischen Sagen beeinflußt war. 4) Für kulturübergreifende Variationen des Schlangenthemas beschäftigte ich mich mit afrikanischer Folklore. In einer Hausa-Fassung ist die Moral in einer Umkehrung impliziert – die Schlange ist nicht dankbar, daß sie gerettet wurde, und alles läuft schief. S. z.B. *Ingratitude* in *Yes and No: The Intimate Folklore of Africa*, von Alta Jablow. Greenwood Press, 1973; Westport, Connecticut. Erstmals veröffentlicht 1961 von Horizon Press, New York. Copyright © 1961 Alta Jablow. In diesem Sinne bei Aesop als *Der Bauer und die Schlange*.

Das Geschenk

Diese ist meine Neufassung einer alten indianischen Sage mit Coyote, Iktome, Fox, bzw. einer Kombination aus ihnen. 1) Von den White River Sioux, *Coyote, Iktome and The Rock* aus *American Indian Myths and Legends*, ausgewählt und hg. von Richard Erdoes und Alfonso Ortiz. Pantheon Books, New York. Copyright © 1984

Random House Inc. Copyright © 1984 Richard Erdoes and Alfonso Ortiz. In their story, Coyote gives his blanket to Iya, the rock. 2) There is another version which features Iktome giving his blanket to Inyan. This is a Dakotas story, called "Iktome's Blanket" from *Old Indian Legends*, retold by Zitkala-Ša. Forword by Agnes M. Picotte. Published by University of Nebraska Press, Lincoln and London. This First Bison Book printing: 1985. Foreword copyright © 1985 by the University of Nebraska Press. Reprinted from the original edition published in 1901, by Ginn; Boston. 3) And then there is the Salish-Blackfoot tale retold by Dee Brown, called "Coyote and the Rolling Rock," in *Dee Brown's Folktales of the Native American*. Published by Henry Holt and Company, Inc., New York. Copyright © 1979, 1993 by Dee Brown. In Dee Brown's version, it's the buddy tale of Coyote and Fox and their meeting with a rock, who remains nameless—but this time witches are involved.

Blind Man's Bluff

My story is based on two versions of the folktale "Daughter and Stepdaughter," collected by the ethnographer Aleksandr Afanas'ev, who released a selection of folktales in serial publication from 1855 to 1864. I read two translations from his original Russian: 1) *Russian Fairy Tales*, collected by Aleksandr Afanas'ev. Translated by Norbert Guterman. Published by Pantheon Books, New York; a division of Random House Inc. Copyright © 1945 Pantheon Books Inc. Copyright renewed © 1973 Random House, Inc. 2) The other translation of the Aleksandr Afanas'ev collection: Natalie Duddington includes "Daughter and Stepdaughter" in her book called *Russian Folk Tales*. First published in the United States, 1969, by Funk & Wagnalls, New York, A Division of Reader's Digest Books, Inc. Copyright © 1969 Natalie Duddington. There are so many differences between these two versions, I consider them to be retellings of the Afanas'ev story, not translations. In my tale, I change genders, making it a contest between two sisters' sons, not the daughters of a father and a stepmother. Rather than creating a contest between the opposing spirits of mouse and bear, I integrate the story of Peter and the Wolf.

Queen of the Jungle

1) General sources: The *Panchatantra*, a collection of Indian literary tales from more than fourteen hundred years ago. 2) Specific sources: I retell a Gujarat story, "The Elephant and The Ant." This has been published in two books that I know of: A) *Folktales of India*, edited by Brenda E. F. Beck, Peter J. Claus, Praphulladatta Goswami, Jawaharlal Handoo. Published by the University of Chicago Press. Copyright © 1987 by The University of Chicago; and B) *Indian Tales*, by Romila Thapar. First published by Penguin Books India (P) Ltd. 1991, now a Puffin Book, reprinted 1992. Copyright © 1991 Romila Thapar. 3) Other sources: In many cultures there are stories of the small victorious over the big. For example, there's a Yoruba tale of "The Bull and the Fly" from *Fourteen Hundred Cowries: Traditional stories of the Yoruba*, collected by Abayomi Fuja. Published by Oxford University Press, London. Copyright © 1962 Oxford University Press. Another variant: a mouse crawls into the Elephant's brain, in "The Mouse who battled the Elephant" from *Mongolian Folktales*, by Hilary Roe Metternich. Published by Avery Press. Copyright © 1996 Avery Press Inc. 4) Notation: All the stories mentioned above are based on conflict between tall and short. There's also the idea of big and small acting selflessly, as in Aesop's fable, "The Lion and The Mouse."

Richard Erdoes und Alfonso Ortiz. In dieser Geschichte gibt Coyote seine Decke an Iya, den Felsen. 2) Es gibt eine andere Fassung in der Iktome seine Decke an Inyan gibt. Dies ist eine Dakota-Geschichte, *Iktome's Blanket* aus *Old Indian Legends*, neu erzählt von Zitkala-Ša. Vorwort von Agnes M. Picotte. University of Nebraska Press, Lincoln und London. Das erste Bison Book: 1985. Copyright Vorwort © 1985 by University of Nebraska Press. Reprint der Originalfassung von 1901, von Ginn, Boston. 3) Und dann gibt es noch eine Salish-Blackfoot-Sage neu erzählt von Dee Brown, *Coyote and the Rolling Rock*, in *Dee Brown's Folktales of the Native American*. Henry Holt and Company, Inc., New York. Copyright © 1979, 1993 by Dee Brown. In Dee Browns Fassung, geht es um die Freundschaft von Coyote und Fox und wie sie auf einen Felsen treffen, der ohne Namen bleibt – aber in dieser Geschichte sind Hexen mit im Spiel.

Blindekuh

Meine Geschichte basiert auf zwei Fassungen der Volkssage *Tochter und Stieftochter*, aufgeschrieben von dem Ethnographen Aleksandr Afanas'ev, der eine Auswahl von Volkssagen von 1855 bis 1864 in regelmäßiger Folge veröffentlicht hat. Ich kenne zwei engl. Übersetzungen aus dem russischen Original: 1) *Russian Fairy Tales*, zusammengestellt von Aleksandr Afanas'ev. Ins Engl. übersetzt von Norbert Guterman. Pantheon Books, New York. Copyright © 1945 Pantheon Books Inc. Copyright erneuert © 1973 Random House, Inc. 2) Die andere Übersetzung: Natalie Duddington hat *Daughter and Stepdaughter* in *Russian Folk Tales* aufgenommen. In den Vereinigten Staaten zuerst 1969 veröffentlicht bei Funk & Wagnalls, New York. Copyright © 1969 Natalie Duddington. Es gibt in diesen Fassungen soviele Unterschiede, daß ich sie als Neufassungen der Afanas'evschen Geschichte betrachte, nicht als Übersetzungen. In meiner Erzählung vertausche ich die Geschlechter und mache daraus einen Wettkampf zwischen den Söhnen der Schwestern, und nicht der Töchter eines Vaters und einer Stiefmutter. Statt dem Wettkampf der konträren Geister Maus und Bär, intergriere ich die Geschichte von Peter und dem Wolf.

Königin des Dschungels

1) Allgemeine Quelle: Das *Panchatantra*, eine Sammlung indischer Erzählungen, die mehr als 1400 Jahre alt sind. 2) Spezifische Quelle: Ich erzähle eine Gujarat-Geschichte nach, *Der Elefant und die Ameise*. Mir sind zwei Bücher bekannt, in denen sie veröffentlicht wurde: A) *Folktales of India*, hg. von Brenda E. F. Beck, Peter J. Claus, Praphulladatta Goswami und Jawaharlal Handoo. University of Chicago Press. Copyright © 1987 by The University of Chicago; und B) *Indian Tales*, von Romila Thapar. Zuerst veröffentlicht von Penguin Books India (P) Ltd., 1991; jetzt ein Puffin Book, reprinted 1992. Copyright © 1991 Romila Thapar. 3) Andere Quellen: Es gibt in vielen Kulturen Geschichten, in denen das Kleine über das Große triumphiert. Zum Beispiel gibt es solch eine Yoruba-Geschichte, *The Bull and the Fly* aus *Fourteen Hundred Cowries: Traditional stories of the Yoruba*, zusammengestellt von Abayomi Fuja. Oxford University Press, London. Copyright © 1962 Oxford University Press. Eine andere Variante: in *The Mouse who battled the Elephant* kriecht eine Maus in das Gehirn eines Elefanten. Aus *Mongolian Folktales*, von Hilary Roe Metternich. Avery Press. Copyright © 1996 Avery Press Inc. 4) Anmerkung: Alle oben genannten Geschichten basieren auf dem Konflikt zwischen Groß und Klein. Es gibt aber auch die Form in der Groß und Klein selbstlos handeln, wie in Aesops Fabel *Der Löwe und die Maus*.

Brothers and Sisters

From Snorri Sturluson's "Edda," the tragic hero Baldr has a blind twin brother who unwittingly kills him. Perhaps I invent the idea of incest with a twin sister (along with a few other changes) to retell this story, I'm not sure. The translation I read: published by Everyman Library in 1987. Reprinted 1996 by J. M. Dent, Orion Publishing Group, London and Charles E. Tuttle Co. Inc.; Rutland, Vermont, USA. Copyright © Introduction, bibliography, indexes and textual editing, David Campbell Publishers. Copyright © 1995 Chronology and Synopsis J. M Dent. In Sturluson's saga, written about 1220, you must piece together different 'chapters' to form the complete narrative. I've read two sources which do so: 1) *Nordic Gods and Heroes*, by Padraic Colum. Published in 1996 by Dover Publications Inc.; Mineola, New York. It is an unabridged and slightly altered republication of the work originally published by The Macmillan Company, New York, in 1920 under the title, *The Children of Odin*. 2) *Myths of the Norsemen: From the Eddas and Sagas*, by H. A. Guerber. Published by Dover Publications Inc. in 1992. This is an unabridged republication of the original publisher: George G. Harrap & Company, London in 1909.

Birth of a Poet

This comes from a Hausa dilemma tale—which I've gathered from various books. 1) In one it's called, "The Man, his Womenfolk, the Well and the Soldier" from *Hausa Tales and Traditions*, an English Translation of *Tatsuniyoyi Na Hausa*, collected by Frank Edgar. Translated and edited by Neil Skinner. Published by Frank Cass & Co. Ltd. Copyright © 1969 Neil Skinner. 2) "Their Eyes Fell Out" is the title of another version and it can be found in *African Folktales: Traditional Stories of the Black World*, selected and retold by Roger D. Abrahams. Published by Pantheon Books, a division of Random House Inc. Copyright © 1983 Roger D. Abrahams. In my story, I change the outcome, the myth and most everything else.

I apologize profusely and humbly if I failed to include credit where due. I will make amends the next time.

Brüder und Schwestern

In Snorri Sturlusons *Edda* hat der tragische Held Baldr einen blinden Zwillingsbruder, der ihn unwissentlich umbringt. Vielleicht ist die Idee des Inzest mit einer Zwillingsschwester (genauso wie ein paar andere Veränderungen) von mir, ich bin mir nicht sicher. Die mir bekannte Übersetzung: Everyman Library, 1987. Reprinted 1996 von J. M. Dent, Orion Publishing Group, London und Charles E. Tuttle Co. Inc., Rutland, Vermont, USA. Copyright © Einleitung, Bibliografie, Index und Bearbeitung, David Campbell Publishers. Copyright © 1995 Chronologie und Synopsis J. M Dent. In Sturlusons Sage, um 1220 geschrieben, muß man die einzelnen ›Kapitel‹ zusammensetzen, um die komplette Geschichte zu bilden. Ich kenne zwei Quellen, die das getan haben: 1) *Nordic Gods and Heroes*, von Padraic Colum. Dover Publications Inc., Mineola, New York, 1996. Dies ist eine unveränderte und erweiterte Ausgabe des Titels *The Children of Odin*, ursprünglich 1920 veröffentlicht von The Macmillan Company, New York. 2) *Myths of the Norsemen: From the Eddas and Sagas*, von H. A. Guerber. Dover Publications Inc., 1992. Dies ist eine unveränderte Neuauflage des Buches der George G. Harrap & Company, London, 1909.

Geburt eines Dichters

Diese kommt von einer Hausa-Erzählung, die ich aus verschiedenen Büchern habe. 1) In dem einen heißt sie *The Man, his Womenfolk, the Well and the Soldier*, in *Hausa Tales and Traditions*, einer engl. Übersetzung von *Tatsuniyoyi Na Hausa*, zusammengestellt von Frank Edgar. Übersetzt und hg. von Neil Skinner. Frank Cass & Co. Ltd. Copyright © 1969 Neil Skinner. 2) *Their Eyes Fell Out* ist der Titel einer anderen Fassung, zu finden in *African Folktales: Traditional Stories of the Black World*, ausgewählt und nacherzählt von Roger D. Abrahams. Panthcon Books. Copyright © 1983 Roger D. Abrahams. In meiner Geschichte verändere ich das Ende, den Mythos und das meiste andere auch.

Ich bitte vielmals und demütig um Verzeihung, falls ich vergessen haben sollte, eine Quelle anzugeben. Ich werde das beim nächsten Mal wiedergutmachen.

SILENT

INSPIRED

KIND

FRUGAL

WICKED

STRONG

BRUTAL

JOYFUL

WILD

ALOOF